"Tell m
look like ~~y~~

She sigh~~ed~~
hair and a ~~perfectly beautiful face. My sisters look~~
just like her. My father was a big, tall, redheaded
man. Unfortunately, I took after him."

"Personally, I think you're the lucky one," Cass
insisted.

"Personally, I think you're the only one in the
world who does." She hoped she was managing to
hide her painful feelings, and tossed out her old
standby: "I'm just a flamingo hatched out in a
nest of swans."

When Cass didn't laugh, she looked up at him,
surprised. "It's supposed to be a joke, Cass."

"Well, it's not to me. You're the most spectacular
woman I've ever seen—"

"I know you don't mean that! I can't stand it
when people try to be kind!"

"You think I'm just being kind? Stormy, when it
comes to my love life, I'm not into charity."

She glanced up, puzzled by the intense tone of
his voice. His expression spurred her heart into a
gallop. His gaze caressed her fiery hair, then
lingered on her lips so long, they began to feel
swollen with the memory of his kiss.

Cass smiled with soft, parted lips. He leaned
forward and touched her lips with his finger.
"You're no flamingo. I'm not sure what a bird of
paradise looks like, but that name fits you a lot
better. You're beautiful, tall and graceful and regal. The fanciest swan would look dowdy next to
you."

She wanted so badly to believe the outrageous
flattery. But it was true—he looked bedazzled. . . .

WHAT ARE *LOVESWEPT* ROMANCES?

They are stories of true romance and touching emotion. We believe those two very important ingredients are constants in our highly sensual and very believable stories in the *LOVESWEPT* line. Our goal is to give you, the reader, stories of consistently high quality that may sometimes make you laugh, sometimes make you cry, but are always fresh and creative and contain many delightful surprises within their pages.

Most romance fans read an enormous number of books. Those they truly love, they keep. Others may be traded with friends and soon forgotten. We hope that each *LOVESWEPT* romance will be a treasure—a "keeper." We will always try to publish

LOVE STORIES YOU'LL NEVER FORGET
BY AUTHORS YOU'LL ALWAYS REMEMBER

The Editors

Joan J. Domning
Stormy's Man

BANTAM BOOKS
NEW YORK · TORONTO · LONDON · SYDNEY · AUCKLAND

STORMY'S MAN

A Bantam Book / January 1992

If you would be interested in receiving protective vinyl
covers for your Loveswept books, please write to this address
for information:

Loveswept
Bantam Books
P.O. Box 985
Hicksville, NY 11802

ISBN 0-553-44155-8

Published simultaneously in the United States and Canada

PRINTED IN THE UNITED STATES OF AMERICA

OPM   0 9 8 7 6 5 4 3 2 1

To Billi Kay, my daughter—
a tall, pretty, very kind Home Health nurse,
who already has a romance hero in her life.

One

Cass Starbaugh glanced at his watch for the tenth time in as many minutes. Three-fourteen P.M. Hilda was forty-four minutes late. He realized it was a sad statement about a perfectly normal unmarried man of twenty-eight when the high points in his life were the visits of a Home Health nurse—especially a middle-aged one who was sort of his aunt to boot.

It was maddening to be restricted with elastic bandages binding his broken upper arm against his healing ribs. He was too big and active a man to enjoy being idle. He needed to be out in the open air, tuning up his heavy equipment for the spring excavating season.

Cass raked the callused fingers of his left hand through his hair and glanced at his watch again. Three-nineteen. Losing all patience, he swept the magazines, books, and brainteasers off the bed with his good arm, and kicked his twisted sheet after them. He gave a frustrated bellow for good measure—wasted effort since he lived alone and his neighbors were well beyond hearing range.

Seconds later he heard a car parking in front of the

house. Usually, Hilda walked right in, but this time she knocked first, then opened the front door and called, "Home Health. Anybody here?" Her voice sounded different, huskier, as if she had a cold.

"Where the hell would I be, when I can't even drive my damn stick-shift pickup with one arm?" he yelled back. "What's with all the formality? Are you afraid of a bare-assed man in a bed all of a sudden?"

He heard her footsteps in the hall, but instead of graying, rotund Hilda, a spectacularly tall woman in her early twenties appeared at Cass's bedroom door. He pulled himself up on the pillows to stare with surprise. Her electric-curly hair was the color of a slightly tarnished penny, so bright it seemed the sun had suddenly lit up his log house. "Well, hello there," he said with a mellow Montana drawl.

"Hi. I assume you're Mr. Starbaugh?" She was studying him warily. Her eyes were an odd light gray with reddish-brown lashes, and her fair skin was freckled.

It was bound to be intimidating for a woman to walk into a strange house and be met by a suggestive greeting from a man of his size, he realized. By way of reassurance he offered a big smile. "Last time I checked I was, except it's Starbaugh with a *buck*, not a *bough*, at the end. But call me Cass. Cass short for nothing, in case you're wondering."

"Okay, Cass it is." Apparently deeming him harmless, she left the safety of the doorway and stepped into the bedroom. "I'm Gayle Stromm."

He tossed back a mispronunciation of his own, hoping to tease the cautious, almost clinical expression out of her eyes. "Gayle Storm? Now that's a fitting name for someone with hair like yours."

Slipping out of her coat, she tapped the name tag fastened to the shoulder of her pale blue turtleneck.

"*Stromm*, not *Storm*," she said crisply, putting the kibosh on his game-playing.

Cass watched with interest as she threw her coat on a chair beside the door and came across the room. She was tall, with legs that went on forever under an above-the-knee denim skirt. He imagined she would fill the arms of a big man like himself just fine. Mmm-hmmm.

She put her large black nurse's bag and clipboard on the table by his bed. "Let's have a look at you and see how things are going, okay?"

"No, it's not okay. Where's Hilda?" Being examined by a woman he'd known all his life was one thing, but Cass didn't relish the idea of this delectable lady looking him over as if he were a side of beef. "Where'd you come from anyway?"

Gayle studied him with questioning eyes. "I'm taking Hilda's place. Didn't she call and tell you?"

"No, she sure as hell didn't."

"She must have forgotten."

"In a pig's eye she did," he muttered, willing to bet his precious backhoe that Hilda had sicced this new nurse on him to pay him back for his teasing. That old bird was smart enough to guess how a woman so lush would affect a man who'd been cooped up a month.

Gayle brushed fiery hair back from her forehead with a wrist. "If you don't think I'll work out as your nurse, I can leave and arrange for someone else to see you."

Cass didn't like the idea of her leaving either. "No, no, that's all right. You might as well stay as long as you're here. What happened to Hilda?"

"Nothing, she gave you to me."

"She *gave* me to you? What am I, the booby prize?"

"Of course not," she said, with not a hint of a smile over his little joke. "She's a supervisor at Home

Health and doesn't usually visit patients at all. The only reason she was seeing you is because one of her nurses is on maternity leave. She hired me to fill in, and thought I might work out for you. That's all there was to it."

Cass stifled a grin when it occurred to him this terribly serious young woman might be even more fun to tease than Hilda. "And what, Miz Stormy Gayle, made the two of you think I wanted some new greenhorn of a nurse taking care of me?"

"I'm not exactly a greenhorn, considering that I worked Critical Care for two years before I came here," she said, her chin coming up and a superior smile quirking up one corner of her mouth. "And with that background in mind, I'll answer the question you asked when I first arrived. No, I'm not afraid of a bare-assed man in a bed. Certainly not when he's mummied in elastic bandages the way you are."

He let his gaze run slowly down over the blue jersey hugging her breasts and the skirt that showed off her shapely legs, then back up to her face. "Well, I don't intend to be mummied forever."

She batted down his semiserious flirtation by saying, "Then it's a moot question, because when you're not mummied any longer, I don't intend to see you in bed."

With that point made clear, she gave him a full smile for the first time. It turned her smoky eyes gentle and warm, and transformed her rather plain face to beautiful. "What scares me worse than a man in bed is this obstacle course of yours." She glanced around at the mess on the floor. "It's a miracle you haven't tripped over it and broken the rest of your bones."

Cass heaved up to a sitting position and peered at the floor. There was the debris he'd kicked off earlier, as well as a dismantled shotgun he'd discovered he couldn't clean with one hand. And bits and pieces of mountain-climbing equipment, interspersed with dirty dishes. "It is pretty bad, isn't it? My cousin's wife brings me dinner. I'll ask her to clean the place up."

"I'm glad you weren't expecting me to do it," she murmured, then let a beat of a pause pass. "I'm a pretty good nurse, but I don't do windows."

The deadpanned quip caught Cass off guard. Her personality was a puzzle, but now he had to suspect she was hiding a real woman behind her professional facade.

For some reason the notion made him remember that all he had on was the bottom half of a set of red thermal underwear, so tight it outlined every damn thing he had. He wasn't particularly modest, but he hated appearing less than dignified and physically fit in front of a woman. Bouncing sideways, he ignored the pain stabbing through his ribs and reached for the sheet on the floor, counterbalancing himself with a knee.

Startled by his sudden dive, Gayle made a grab for his arm. "What happened? Are you falling?"

"No, I'm not falling! I'm not *that* bad off yet." He dragged the sheet up onto the bed. She was still bending over him, and when he'd levered himself back up onto his pillows, they ended up almost nose to nose. Her flowery scent curled around him like a caress.

Their gazes met and held. An odd sense of energy crackled between them, lingering slightly even after she'd looked away and stepped back. There'd always been women in Cass's life, but he'd never had anything like that happen before. It was unsettling, almost scary, to feel such a strong attraction, as if something momentous was about to happen.

He glanced sharply at Gayle, wondering if she'd felt

it too. Apparently she hadn't. Her expression was unreadable as she smoothed her lively hair. Stung by an irrational sense of rejection, he flapped the sheet in place over his body and muttered, "I'm not exactly dressed for company."

"And I'm not exactly company, remember? I've seen male patients dressed in less."

"Not me, you haven't."

She eyed him for a second, then dipped her head to take a blood-pressure cuff and stethoscope out of her bag. "If you quit quibbling, we can get this over with, Mr. Starbaugh."

"I'm Cass, not mister."

"And I'm Ms. Stromm." She sat down on the edge of the bed and tugged at her short skirt a little self-consciously. Then she tucked his wrist between her elbow and body, and wrapped the cuff around his upper arm.

Cass couldn't resist flexing his biceps under her fingers, hoping to point out that three-quarters of his body was still in good shape, honed and well muscled from his climbing. In case she was interested.

She deflated his ego quickly, "Quit showing off, I'm not here for fun and games," she said. After ascertaining that his blood pressure was normal, she removed the cuff and ordered, "Sit up and let me unwind you."

Cass pulled himself upright, hiding a wince of pain. "You're the boss, Miz Stormy, ma'am."

"And don't you forget it," Gayle said, removing the elastic bandages with surprisingly gentle hands.

"I'm sure you won't let that happen," Cass muttered as she poked, prodded, listened to his chest, and asked embarrassing questions about his bodily functions.

Finally, she jotted her findings on the clipboard

and looked up with a smile. "Since you're on the mend, the doctor has okayed a shower with your arm in a sling."

His sagging ego recovered instantly. "Hot damn! You don't know how good that sounds after a month of canary flutters!" He swung his long legs over the side of the bed.

"Hey, not so fast, watch the shoulder." Gayle applied the sling to his arm and buckled the ends around his neck. When he started to get up, she put her hands on his shoulders to hold him down. "Will you quit being so jumpy! Wait here until I get everything ready."

She nosed out a gray terry robe, towels, and a clean thermal bottom, and put everything in the master bath. Then she came back to the bed and took his good arm to help him up. "Whoa, you're a big one, aren't you?" she said when he was on his feet.

"A keeper, one of my uncles used to say." The top of her head was level with his mouth, which meant she was damn near six feet tall herself. "You're a keeper, too, it seems."

She turned quickly away. "I guess, at least no one's thrown me back yet."

Cass surmised from the defiant tone in her voice that she didn't feel comfortable with her extra inches, though they looked spectacular to him as he watched her clear a path through the litter, her long legs moving gracefully and her breasts swaying under the snug jersey. She carried herself straight and proud, not hunched over the way some tall women tended to do.

He let her help him to the bathroom and heat up the shower, but he rebelled when she reached for the waistband of his thermals. "Look, boss or no boss, I can undress myself!" Any other time he would have leaped at the chance to have a woman strip him, but not when his chest was caved in, he was covered with bruises, and he couldn't do anything about her.

"Oh, don't be so prudish. This is your first shower since the accident, and I want to be sure you're steady on your legs. I don't particularly relish the idea of writing an incident report, if you take a nosedive." With that, she hooked her fingers in his elastic waistband and stripped his thermals down over his hips and legs. Without so much as turning a hair. Just as if she went around bulldogging naked men every day. Which she probably did, he realized. That notion didn't please him.

"Lift your feet so I can get these off," she ordered, adding after a beat, "one at a time."

He lifted his feet as directed, irritated because she made him feel like an adolescent, worried that he'd embarrass himself with an impromptu erection. Perversely, it annoyed him that she didn't seem interested enough to so much as glance at his privates. He strode into the shower and slammed the door.

Cass's shower was custom-built so that he could soak the full six feet six inches of his battered body under a heavenly, hot, cleansing spray. At least it would have been heaven if one incomprehensible redhead hadn't been hovering around outside, germinating a sense of hunger in him that food would never satisfy.

To make things worse, when he came out, she impersonally rubbed him dry with the towels and wrapped him in his terry robe. Then she held the clean red thermals for him to step into.

After that, Cass was beyond fighting anything she did. He meekly let her bundle him back into his bed, which she'd made up with fresh, clean sheets. After redressing his chest wound and immobilizing his arm against his ribs once again, she began packing her things back into her bag. "Last chance," she said.

"Do you have any problems the doctor and I should know about?"

"Problems? I guess not." Outside of the fact that he felt as if she'd shaken him out and snapped him straight, like a damp dish towel.

"If any medical problems come up, call me." She jotted her number on a slip of paper and stuck the edge under the base of the lamp. Then she walked toward her coat on the chair by the door.

As disconcerting as the woman was, Cass didn't want her to leave. He'd be alone and bored again. Besides, he was curious about the person behind the facade, and scrambled to start a conversation. "Do you have any other patients to see after you leave here?"

She shook her head, slipping her arms into the sleeves of her light beige coat. "No, I'll touch base at Home Health, and then I'm off duty."

"Why don't you stay a while and keep me company? I've got a bottle of wine in the fridge, if you don't mind opening it yourself."

"Thanks, but I like to keep professional relationships just that." She smiled to take the sting out of her refusal, and buttoned the one large button on the tapered coat.

Cass wasn't accustomed to women turning him down; she was one tough challenge. He lowered his dark brows. "You asked if I had any problems. I do. I've got a fever."

Her lips twitched, as if she'd heard it all before. "I took your temperature a few minutes ago, and you didn't have a fever," she said as she picked up her bag.

"Yes, I do. Cabin fever. It's bad enough that winter is lasting forever, without being terminally housebound and bored out of my gourd."

She glanced around the bedroom. "How can you

possibly be bored with such an amazing display of recreational therapy spread all over your floor?"

He muttered a blue-tinged comment about recreational therapy. "I'm going nuts! I need to go back to work."

Gayle stood hip-shot, holding her bag in front of her legs. "What do you do?"

"Dig holes and move dirt."

Her face came to life when she laughed. "What kind of holes?"

Cass heaved himself up off the pillows and leaned forward, gratified to see he'd finally lit a spark of interest in her eyes. "I dig anything—ditches, trenches—but mostly basements for new houses. I'm the C in C and J Excavating. The J is Jackson, he's sort of my brother." He waved his hand toward the window. "Those are my babies out there."

She walked across the room to look out at the heavy equipment in three separate, oversize garages. There was a bulldozer, a backhoe, a flatbed truck, and a dump truck, and his everyday upgraded, blue-and-chrome pickup. "Very impressive."

He smiled self-mockingly to cover his pride. "Big boys' toys. I loved the sandbox so much when I was a kid, I couldn't give it up. I'd hate to admit how much fun I have running those machines—ripping things up and rearranging the earth. I like reshaping the yards after the houses are finished, especially if they're on a hill. It's like creating a work of art. I guess I must be a frustrated landscaper at heart." He broke off, realizing he was talking too much again, and half-embarrassed over his flight toward fancy.

But she seemed to understand, and nodded. "Yes, I imagine it must be fun. I'll bet you'd love my yard. It's a funny shape, too long side to side, too narrow in depth, and on a steep hill. Nothing has ever been done to it, and it's covered with a jungle of winter-killed knapweed."

"Sounds like you could use some railroad ties or a rock garden."

"I probably could, but I don't have the time or the money for anything so elaborate." She hefted her bag and walked back to the door.

Cass swung his legs over the side of the bed and sat up, scrabbling to extend the conversation. "You must have just moved here, I haven't seen you around before."

Gayle stopped and looked at him. "And I suppose you know everyone in town?"

"Just about. After all the population is only about three thousand, and I've lived here since I was eight."

She nodded. "You're right. I came from Portland three weeks ago."

He grinned. "Welcome to Hamilton and the beautiful Bitterroot Valley, ma'am."

Her face lit up in a smile, and she dipped a little bow. "Thank you, sir, but the welcome is a little premature. My stay here is only temporary. I'm going home in three months. That's when my leave of absence from my real job is up."

Cass felt his heart drop at that news; his attraction to her was becoming annoying. He considered rela-tionships to be unreliable, generally, so it ought to have relieved him to see Ms. Stormy Gayle holding him at bay and champing at the bit to leave town. But it didn't, it irritated him. "Why'd you come to Hamilton then, if you aren't staying?"

"It's a complicated story. I'm remodeling a little old fixer-upper house for sale."

"That sounds like a hell of a lot of hard work," he said, hinting for an explanation so he could fit another piece into the puzzle that was her personal-ity.

"Not really. It's different from my usual grind, and I needed a break." She waggled her fingers in a good-bye wave and walked out of the bedroom.

Cass got up as fast as he could and waged a one-armed battle to drape his robe over his shoulders, clutching the sides shut in front. By the time he made it to the living room, Gayle had her hand on the front doorknob. He grabbed at an old standby to hold her: "How's the weather? Is it cold out?"

She glanced back. "A little chilly, but not bad for March. The sun's been out all day and melted some of the snow."

"That sounds hopeful. My doctor won't let me go out on the ice and snow with only one good arm. So here I am, stuck in the house."

She hesitated sympathetically for a moment, then took pity on him and came back to meander around the living room, like a stray sunbeam livening up the bleak atmosphere. She looked at the squared cedar walls, the vaulted ceiling, and the freestanding plank stairway to the second floor. She admired the original Thornbrough bird paintings and the Russell Wild West prints. "At least you have a very beautiful home to be stuck in," she said, smiling.

"Thanks, but I only moved in six months ago, and it's still a house, not a home yet." He glanced around with vague dissatisfaction at the masculine decorating. He'd picked up the environmental colors of the outdoors, blues, grays,and golden beige. "It needs a special touch to give it life, but I can't figure out what."

"Looks fine to me." She gazed out the window. "You have quite a view. I can even see my little house."

Cass walked across the room and dutifully looked at the horses and beef cattle making trails through the snow in the pastures below the hill. The town was beyond the pastures, and the mountains beyond that. But he was more interested in her tall, generous body than the view. It was quite a novelty to stand behind a women he didn't dwarf. "Where is this house of yours?"

"Over there, about two miles across the valley on that square ridge at the base of the mountains. It's painted such a ghastly shade of yellow, it jumps out at you."

"Right, I see it." He grinned and drawled, "That's handy, Miz Stormy Gayle. If I need a nurse, I'll send up a flare and you'll come running."

She made a face at him. "You're acting less feeble by the minute, so don't count on it."

"What happened to your bedside manner?"

"I left it back at your bedside."

"Now, there's an interesting thought." He quickly changed the subject when she gave him a narrow-eyed look. "You must have some view yourself, over there."

"I suppose I do, but I'm too busy to look at it," she said. "Besides, having mountains towering on every side makes me feel claustrophobic. I'm used to Portland and looking at just a peak or two on the horizon, where they belong."

"Claustrophobic! What an idea," Cass said. "You ought to get out in the mountains, climb one." A prickle of nervous perspiration broke out on his forehead and chest as he frowned at the nine-thousand footers across the valley. Their snow-covered peaks were piercing through the clouds into a pristine blue sky. "There's good climbing in the Bitterroot Range. Not the best in the country, but pitting oneself against some of them can be a contest."

Gayle glanced at his bound arm making a bulge under his robe. "It wasn't much of a contest last time you pitted yourself against them. Mark up one for the mountain and nothing for you—except a concussion, four broken ribs, a punctured lung, and a hairline fracture of the right humerus."

"I'll admit it wasn't particularly humorous at the time." He gave a twisted smile when she groaned over his play on words. "Actually, I wasn't mountain climbing, I was rock climbing in Blodgett Canyon."

"What's the difference?"

Cass forced himself to look across the valley at the canyon. It was a great gash between two mountains, lined by vertical cliffs. Suppressing a shudder, he turned his back to the window. "Mountain climbing is with ropes and pitons. Rock climbing is with fingernails and toenails."

Gayle gave him an acid look. "Then if you were rock climbing, it makes your accident even more nonsensical, doesn't it?"

First he lifted his chin, ready to take offense, but then he realized she wasn't aware of how he had gotten into the situation. "That depends," he hedged, perfectly willing to be as unreasonable and stubborn as she.

"Depends on what?" When he didn't answer, she cocked her head questioningly. "I honestly believe you intend to go right back up there as soon as you've healed, don't you?"

His climbing was almost as important to him as his excavating business. At least it had been until the accident. "Yes . . . I do intend to. I have to," he said, his jaw knotting. "Someday."

Cass had never in his life been afraid of anything. But now a knot of fear twisted his stomach when he thought about going back up. It was too embarrassing to admit his fear to himself; he certainly didn't want an attractive woman to guess. Mustering a grin, he tried to make light of it. "Don't tell me you're worried about my poor, tender hide."

Gayle jerked one shoulder up, anger flashing in her smoky eyes. "I suppose it's none of my business what you do with your hide, but I can't help seeing it as totally ridiculous for you to risk life and limb for a cheap thrill!" Whirling around, she marched out of the house and closed the door with a fraction more force than necessary.

Cass gaped at the blank door, trying to figure out what had triggered her anger. But it was obvious she thought he was a reckless fool, which was only minimally preferable to having her guess he'd turned into a raving coward. He jumped when the door burst open again after a few seconds.

"I came back to apologize," Gayle said, lighting up his house with her windblown copper hair. "I was out of line in overreacting to your climbing."

"I suppose you might have had a point," Cass conceded, "considering why you came here in the first place." He was so pleased that she'd come back with even a grudging peace offering that he forgot and gave a generous shrug. Then he grunted and slipped his hand under his robe to press the stab of pain in his ribs.

"Are you all right?" she asked, stepping forward.

The last thing his battered dignity needed was Ms. Professional tossing him around again. He straightened up and forced a smile to hide the pain. "Never mind! I'm fine," he insisted, then whispered, "*Damn!*" when his robe slipped off his shoulders to pool around his bare feet.

"If you're sure . . . ?" Gayle eyed him a moment longer before turning to the door.

She paused with her hand on the knob and glanced back over her shoulder. A big grin lit up her face. "Love your 'jammies, Mr. Macho." The instant she said it, a raging blush flared up to obliterate the

generous scatter of freckles under her creamy skin.
The next instant she'd popped out of sight.

Cass let go of his ribs and snapped the waistband
of his tight thermals. The real Ms. Professional Gayle
was still a puzzle, but apparently she wasn't quite as
objective about him as she'd tried to pretend. And
that suited him just fine. He also liked it that she had
a sense of humor after all, though he sure as hell
hated being made the butt of it.

"Just you wait, lady," he muttered. "Your day is
coming. Mmm-hmm!"

Two

Gayle ran down the porch steps of Cass Starbaugh's rustically elegant log house and climbed into her car. Her hands were shaking, her breath speeding, her heart thumping a rhumba—all the signs of a fight or flight reaction.

Or of an impossibly inopportune attraction, she realized with a sinking sensation. Cass Starbaugh was a playboy in the literal sense of the word, considering the way he talked about his oversize toys. Not to mention his climbing. It was ridiculous to feel so drawn to him, when she took pride in her strong sense of social responsibility.

Heat burned her cheeks when she thought about her parting remark: *Love your 'jammies.* After the shower scene he was bound to know she'd seen exactly what he had filling out those red thermals. "How Freudianly idiotic can you get!" she muttered, jamming the key into the ignition. What on earth had caused her to say such a thing?

Only a moment's thought produced an answer to her question: For the first time since the age of thirteen she'd felt small and delicate with a man, instead of oversized and gawky. Even bandaged and bruised, Cass radiated strength, with broad shoulders, a waist like a tree trunk, and legs even longer than hers. She'd actually had to look *up* into his face. It'd taken every ounce of her professional control to hide her reaction to him. At least she had until the end.

Starting the engine with a roar, Gayle drove down the hill and through Hamilton. The downtown buildings, built around the turn of the century, resembled those of the Old West. But the hospital, where she parked her compact, was modern brick and glass. Plodding down the hall to the Home Health Department, she knocked on Hilda Westerman's open door.

Her supervisor looked up and smiled. "Come in and sit down. Tell me all about your first day on your own."

Gayle put her bag and clipboard down on the single chair in the office. Perching on the edge of the desk, she wound one leg around the other and said, "Not so bad. My first two patients were fairly routine. The third, Harvey Fenster, nearly talked my arm and leg off, old curmudgeon that he is. But I think we'll get along all right."

She took a breath and blew it out. "Cass Starbaugh was something else again. You must have forgotten to let him know I was coming. I think it shook him up to have a stranger walk in on him."

A sly smile crept across Hilda's round face. "I'll just bet it did. I love that young man dearly, but I honestly hope the shock of having you pop in shut his mouth for him. For *once.*"

Gayle inspected her nails. "He wasn't the one who lost his cool. I lost mine." She lifted her shoulders and glanced up. "Maybe it'd be better if someone else saw him next time."

"Oh, no! Cass's got all my other nurses buffaloed. I

was hoping with your heavy-duty background, you could handle him and give me a break from his devilment." Hilda shook her head and sighed. "What'd he say to you?"

"That wasn't it—I didn't take anything he said personally. He's so bored, he'd tease anyone coming within range."

"Oh? He wouldn't let you take care of him then, is that it?"

"No, I railroaded over his objections and did what he needed to have done."

A glint lit Hilda's eyes. "Good for you! Serves him right. What *is* the problem then?"

Gayle frowned, trying to think of a delicate way to explain. An image of Cass rose in her mind. His face was burned permanently tan by the weather, his sandy hair sun-streaked and falling in a tousled wing above laughing brown eyes. She ran her fingers into the coppery hair over her forehead and grimaced the memory away. "I'm embarrassed to admit it, but I think my libido may have become involved."

"Oh, don't let that bother you! At least half the women in the valley admit to sacrificing their libidos to Cass, either in fact or fantasy," Hilda said, and added picturesquely from her ranch background, "I just wish one of them had corralled and ringed him, so I wouldn't have this nursing problem. But he's spooky as a yearling colt about letting himself be lassoed."

Gayle snorted a laugh. "I hope you're not suggesting I join in the roundup. All those twinkly little women would stampede right over me."

"I wouldn't be too sure about that, you're no ugly duckling."

"Not an ugly duckling, no, just a flamingo hatched out in a nest of swans. See, I've even got the honker for it." She grinned and touched her modest Roman nose. "I grew up, and up, the middle child between two pretty, poised sisters, so I learned early on to be realistic about myself." Her tone was light, covering the fact that she wasn't as tough as she'd like people to think. "I've met men like Cass before. He'd flirt with a department store dummy, until a better prospect appeared."

"Is *that* why you don't want to go back? Did he get too friendly?"

"Of course not. He's full of hot air. I got a kick out of his foolishness."

Hilda let out an exasperated breath. "Would you kindly let me in on what the problem was?"

Gayle lowered her brows thoughtfully. "I guess he bothers me, because I liked him. Which makes it twice as hard to stomach that damn mountain climbing of his." The muscles in her shoulders and neck tightened at the thought of it.

"Ah," Hilda said softly. "Why didn't I guess, knowing your background? Would it help to talk about it?"

"I don't see how it could. But the simple fact is that I spent two years in the business of picking up the pieces. I saw too much blood and guts in Critical Care to sympathize with a man who'd risk life and limb on something so useless as climbing a mountain."

Gayle unwound her legs and paced around the small office to air her frustrations. "It gives me the creeps to think of Cass Starbaugh climbing up a vertical cliff again. Life is so precious. Why doesn't he respect his?"

"Are you sure he doesn't?" Hilda asked, her forehead creased.

"I only know how it looks."

The tension had begun to ease out of Gayle's neck. "I guess I do feel better. Thanks for letting me spout off."

"Good, do you think you could see Cass again?"

"Oh, I suppose. He's healing so fast, he should need only one more visit anyway. After that, we can both go on our merry little ways, in different directions, and I won't have to worry about what he's doing." Or about the impractical yearnings he'd sparked.

"And the different direction I want to head in is back to Portland to pick up my life again. So I'd better go home and get that house of my mother's fixed up." She picked up her big black bag and walked to the door.

Loneliness was the worst part, Gayle decided that evening. She hadn't made any friends yet, and probably wouldn't in the short time she meant to stay in the valley. She was standing on a stepladder in her remodeling ensemble—tattered jeans, a sweatshirt, and old canvas shoes—rollering white paint on the ceiling of a bedroom.

At 8:00 P.M. the pathetic little house seemed to hulk around her, with blackness pressing in outside the windows. Not even lively tape music could stave off the eerie, small-town night silence. "I'll know things are really bad when I start talking to myself," she muttered, squinting against a spray of fine white droplets.

As she climbed down off the ladder to refill her paint pan a few minutes later, a flash caught the corner of her vision. Cupping her hands around her face, she looked curiously out the window. The black sky was peppered with a billion stars. Below the hill neon signs marked downtown, and all the streets were mapped by streetlights.

She drew in a surprised breath when a streak of light shot up across the valley and burst into a blossom of red sparks. Another streak went up, wobbling off at a different angle, and blossomed into a circle of blue. "Now why would some idiot be setting off fireworks in March?" she asked, then laughed with delight as several rockets went up in rapid succession.

When the show was over, Gayle filled her pan and climbed the ladder. She'd only made one swipe with the roller when the phone rang. Climbing down again, she ran to the kitchen and grabbed up the receiver, noticing too late that her hand was smeared with paint. "Hello!" she said, anticipating a call from her mother.

"Well, hello there, Miz Gayle Stromm." It was the deep voice of a big man.

A few beats of surprised silence passed. "Is that you, Cass?" she asked, though the identity behind the drawl was no mystery. Her heart began to beat faster, to her disgust.

"Sure it's me. Why didn't you come running?"

"What *are* you talking about?"

"I told you this afternoon that I'd send up flares if I needed you."

"You mean *you're* the idiot shooting off skyrockets?" she exclaimed, laughing.

"The very one." His answering laugh rumbled in her ear. "I was afraid you hadn't seen them."

"I did, I loved them. But where did you get fireworks in the winter? I thought they were illegal."

"Leftovers from last Fourth, and not in Montana they aren't."

"You're lucky you didn't blow the fingers off your good hand."

He clicked his tongue. "You must be the worst fussbudget in the entire Northwest Territory."

Gayle rubbed her sweatshirt sleeve across her face, trying to erase a grin; it was folly to let herself be charmed by him. "You'd better be calling about a legitimate problem, Cass."

"I am, I'm lonesome."

"Since when is loneliness a medical emergency?" She leaned her hips against the cracked, stained Formica counter and stretched out her long legs.

"Oh, come on, Stormy, don't be unfriendly."

"I thought I was Ms. Stromm. Where'd you come up with this Stormy business?"

"It seems fitting, the way you whipped me around like a hurricane this afternoon," he said. "Listen, one of my grandmothers brought me some nibbles to go with that bottle of wine. Why don't you come on over and share them with me?"

Gayle glanced around. The kitchen, dining, and living rooms opened into each other, and were furnished with what appeared to be secondhand-store rejects. The space seemed so silent and lonely, she barely managed to resist temptation. "I told you, Cass, I don't mix business and pleasure."

"Then you *do* consider having wine with me a pleasure?"

"Figuratively, not literally," she said, smiling and struggling to keep all humor out of her voice. "Besides, I'm busy."

"With what? A date?"

"I don't think that's any of your business."

"Maybe not, but if you're entertaining some local dude, I'll hear all about it tomorrow anyway. Small town grapevines being what they are."

"Oh, that's comforting. But as it so happens, I'm up on a stepladder, painting a ceiling."

"Right now? You've got me hanging from the ceiling?"

"No, you brought me down to earth with your call." Her smile died when she realized how far that statement was from the truth; just the sound of his voice had sent her up like one of his rockets. "The point I'm trying to make is that I'm busy, Cass. My paint is drying out. I've got to go spread it."

"How'd you get rooked into a job like painting?"

"It's a long story."

"I'm not rushing off anywhere."

She hesitated, then gave in. "Well, my uncle retired in Hamilton about, oh, a year and a half ago, and—"

"How'd he happen to find this little old place?" Cass interrupted.

"This little place has a reputation. *The Wall Street Journal* mentioned the Bitterroot Valley as a prime retirement site. He bought this house, then upped and died before he could fix it up, much less enjoy it. He willed it to my mother, and she wants to sell it. So I came here to fix it up."

"And to bring a ray of sunshine into my life."

"I wouldn't know about that." Pleasure warmed her face, though Gayle knew his tongue was probably so glib through years of practice.

"Remodeling isn't any bed of roses. Could you use a hand to help you? I know a pretty good one that's available. I may not be able to drive with one hand, but I sure could manage a paintbrush. If you want to pick me up, that is."

When Gayle realized she was on the verge of accepting his offer, she clamped her teeth together. Something odd seemed to happen to her around Cass, a melting of her better judgment. That's all you need, she thought to herself, a romantic disaster to complicate your Critical Care burnout. "I appreciate your offer, but I have to take care of this myself," she said firmly. "I'm going to hang up now."

She pressed the disconnect button before she could change her mind. Then she stood holding the receiver, listening to the silence and emptiness of the house pressing around her. When she found herself looking at the buttons, half-tempted to dial Cass back, she exclaimed, "What are you thinking of!"

She slapped the receiver onto the cradle, but it was stuck to the paint on her hand. Peeling off her fingers one by one, she felt like a fly trying to escape a sticky web, with the spider waiting and smiling. "That man is making me crazy," she said, giving a shaky laugh.

On Wednesday afternoon Gayle first visited old Harvey Fenster out in the country, then drove back into town and parked in front of Cass's house. Getting out of the car, she smoothed the French braid confining her rebellious hair to the back of her head. "You can do this," she whispered to herself. "You're a professional, and he's a patient. He's sick, he's hurt. Just go in there and do your job. Nothing to it. Cuppa tea."

Taking a deep breath, she walked up onto the porch and knocked, then opened the door and called out, "Home Health."

No answer. The house was quiet. Too quiet. Something was wrong.

She rushed to Cass's bedroom. The floor had been picked up, but the sheets on his bed were rumpled and thrown back. An open magazine was turned facedown on the bedside table. Cass wasn't there. He wasn't in the bathroom either. She dropped her bag and ran through the rest of the house. He wasn't anywhere.

Frowning with worry, she walked back to his bedroom and looked at his bed. He must have forgotten I was coming, she thought to herself. The idea hurt a little. Or had he had a setback and been taken to the hospital? Her heart thumped as a dozen possible medical complications leaped to mind.

Hilda would know; Gayle grabbed up the phone. Then she put the receiver down without dialing when she glanced out the window and saw a flash of red—Cass's cap. He was ambling from one garage to another. Relief surged over her body.

She ran through the house, out the door, and around to the backyard. A crow in a giant, leafless cottonwood tree jeered at her passing. There wasn't much snow left in the yard, and the path to the garages was soft and spongy, muffling her footsteps. In the middle garage Cass had his head bent over the engine of the backhoe and didn't hear her approach.

It gave Gayle the freedom to look him over. She'd remembered him as being big, but in his clothes he looked like a veritable Paul Bunyan. His blue plaid flannel shirt was open at the neck and rolled up at the sleeves over a red thermal top. His faded jeans were held up by red suspenders, the bottoms tucked into high-top work boots.

His right arm was in a sling, and he was idly squeezing a rubber ball to rebuild his muscles, but he didn't look a bit like the sickly patient she'd psyched herself up to visit. It irritated her to see him looking so healthy, when she'd been so worried. "Aren't you supposed to be in the house recuperating?" she demanded curtly.

Surprise shot him up out of the engine. His grin was irresistible, pushing creases into his cheeks. "Well, hello to you, too, Miz Stromm. Good to see you, and how are you?"

"Okay, okay. Hi, Cass, good to see you," she said with an answering smile. "Sorry I snapped at you, but you scared me. I thought something had happened to you, when I couldn't find you in the house."

He pulled the bill of his red cap low over twinkling brown eyes. "Why, I didn't know you cared."

"It's my job to care," she said airily, waving a hand.

"What *are* you doing out here anyway? And where are your elastic bandages?"

He lifted the ball in his right fingertips. "I went to the doctor yesterday. He let me out of prison and put me on parole."

She cocked her head. "Don't try to tell me he said you could come out here and work on these monsters of yours."

"Well, he didn't exactly say I could, but he didn't say I couldn't either."

"Because you didn't ask."

"Well, maybe I didn't." He gave the side of the huge yellow backhoe a slap. It looked clean and lovingly attended, with its jointed arm folded, scoop tucked against its breast. "I'm not really working, I just came out to say hello to my babies."

Gayle crossed her arms and shifted her weight to one foot. "If you're in such wonderful shape, then why am I here?"

He lifted his cap, brushed back his sun-streaked hair, and settled it again, all done one-handed. "Because you wanted to see me?" He glanced teasingly at her.

She smiled, thinking the fact that he was right should be construed as dangerous. "You should have called Home Health and canceled my visit."

"A month of boredom might have driven me nuts, but not crazy," he said, hooking his thumb in a red suspender. "*I* wanted to see you, so why would I cancel your visit?"

"But wanting isn't needing, so I'd better go."

"Oh, I need you, Stormy, mmm-hmmm."

His grin made her feel quivery inside. "You really are impossible, Cass," she said, her voice huskier than usual.

"Yea-ah," he said, drawing out the word seductively. "So I've been told."

The intimation that he routinely teased women snapped her back to her senses. "Since you're up and about, it's a waste of time for me to stay." She turned around to walk out of the garage.

When Cass walked beside her down the path, shortening his steps to match hers, she felt again that sense of being delicate and dainty. She felt like a stranger to herself, a woman she'd never been before. She didn't enjoy the feeling. No, that wasn't true; she was frightened of the feeling, because she could so easily grow to enjoy it too much.

"Why don't you come inside and visit for a few minutes?" he asked, when they came around to the front of the house.

"You never give up, do you?" she said. "I'm still on duty. I have to go back to the hospital and report in. I'm sure Hilda has other patients for me to see in your place."

Cass did something tricky with the ball in his right fingers, and ended up pointing a forefinger at her. "I'll bet dollars to doughnuts I'm going to pay for this visit anyway. You owe me at least an hour of your time."

Gayle gave a laugh. "That's the silliest rationale I've ever heard."

"It was the best I could come up with on short notice," he said, thumbing the bill of his cap up to a cocky angle. "Let me try this one—I've still got that bottle of wine. Wouldn't it be fun to get to know each other a little better?"

"Hilda will be wondering what happened to me," she insisted, reminding herself, not him.

"Oh, forget Hilda, she's sort of my aunt, so I'll make it right with her." The sparkle in his brown eyes indicated that he knew he was wearing her down. "Let's try another rationale. Since I don't need your professional services any longer, you don't have to worry about mixing business and pleasure."

"I don't have time for pleasure, I need every spare minute to remodel my house." She began striding toward the driveway, hoping to be able to resist him long enough to reach the sanctuary of her car. Once she drove away, she'd never have to see him again.

"If you don't have time for fun, then what's the use of living?" he asked, striding along beside her.

"That's your philosophy, not mine. Maybe some of us have a stronger sense of responsibility than others of us."

"Now that's an even sillier rationale than mine."

Gayle felt weak by the time she crawled in behind the steering wheel. But her relief was short-lived. "Damn!" she whispered, and glanced through the open car door at Cass. "My keys are in my bag, and I left that in your house."

"Then you'll just have to come on inside and get it, won't you?" he drawled, a smug grin twitching at his lips.

She laughed. "I suppose you think you've won, smarty."

He agreed with a breathy, drawn-out "Yea-ah."

Gayle got out of the car and walked beside Cass to the front door. He held it open, and she went into the living room and frowned. When she remembered where she'd left her Home Health bag, she decided the fates must be conspiring against her. "I guess I left it in your bedroom."

"Uh-huh, in my bedroom." He put a world of meaning in his simple comment.

"I can get it myself—you stay here," she said, pointing forcefully at the floor before marching down the hall.

Flitting skittishly into his bedroom, Gayle grabbed her bag. When she turned, she discovered Cass hadn't followed orders. His shoulders filled the doorway, his head almost touched the frame at the top. His face was serious, with a slight inviting curve on his lips. His eyes were warm with an age-old question. Even the way his fingers were gently kneading the ball was suggestive.

Gayle's gaze flicked toward the huge rumpled bed and back at him. Even half-healed, Cass was one man she wasn't big enough to best if he decided to turn the situation into a tussle. Taking a deep breath, she stepped forward, clutching her bag in front of her. He didn't move.

"Let me through, Cass," she said, pressing a forefinger against his blue plaid shirt at the exact middle of his broad chest. To her immense relief the gentlest pressure moved him backward as she stepped forward.

The tiny smile on his lips grew as she slipped past him. He'd left so little room in the doorway that her breasts brushed his sling. The ball dropped to bounce on the floor as he closed his fingers around her forefinger on his chest, stopping her. "You look terrified—what did you think I was going to do?"

"How should I know what you'd do?" she said. "I don't know anything about you." To her dismay his nearness sent excitement scampering through her body, replacing the anxiety.

His gaze read and caressed her face. "One of these days you'll know me well enough to beg for my bed and me in it."

"Don't hold your breath." She pulled her finger free and slipped away from him.

Cass bent over to retrieve his ball. Coming up too fast, he sagged against the wall. "It appears I wouldn't have had enough spice and vinegar to do anything to you, even if I had wanted to."

Gayle felt a rush of concern when she saw his pale

face. She went back to put her arm around his waist. "Here, I'll help you lie down on your bed."

"Now, don't you start throwing your weight around again," he said, pressing her backward into the living room. "I can recuperate just as well in here."

He sat down on the puffy gray leather sofa, his red cap toppling off as he dropped his head back. "But I'm afraid you'll have to open the wine yourself."

She leaned over and curled her fingers around his massive wrist to take his pulse. It was strong and steady. "If you drank a drop of wine, you'd be flat on your back."

His color was coming back, and his grin was impudent. "Good idea, Stormy. We'll save the wine until I'm capable and you're submissive."

"Dream on, Starbaugh."

"I will, you can count on it. But for the time being, will you kindly quit hovering over me? Sit *down*."

"Maybe just for a minute, until I'm sure you're all right." She opened her coat and perched on the edge of a blue tweed easy chair. "I hope next time you pay attention to your doctor and let things heal before you go pushing bulldozers around."

"Yeah, well . . ." He stretched out his long legs and crossed them at the ankles. "Sorry I wasn't in the house when you came, but you were early."

She gave a wry laugh. "That's because the patient I saw before you kicked me out."

"That'd be old Harvey Fenster."

Her brows shot up. "How did you know?"

"He's sort of a great-uncle of mine, so I call him every now and then to see how he's getting along. What'd you say to make him kick you out?"

"Well, he doesn't take care of himself—I suggested he think about nursing homes."

Cass snorted a laugh. "No wonder! Old Harvey still

has every penny he ever pinched. He'd never fork a one of them out for something like that."

She laughed too. "So he told me, in no uncertain terms."

Cass was silent a moment, studying her face. "There's something I'm more curious about than Harvey. Here you are on your own, a girl of only twenty, it seems—"

"I'm not a girl, I'm twenty-four."

"Oh, are you now? I wondered." He laughed when she made a face. "Okay, here you are, a woman of only twenty-four. It still seems funny your mother would send you out into the middle of nowhere to remodel her house. Why didn't she hire someone?"

"It wasn't her idea, it was mine," she said, her smile fading. "My father divorced her a few years back. She barely makes ends meet, so the money from the sale of the house will mean a lot to her. My sisters anted up some funds for remodeling, and I offered to come and do the job. Or do what I can, and organize the rest some way or another."

He searched her face for a few seconds. "It's awfully nice of you to give up a big chunk of your life for her."

"It wasn't all that noble. I needed some R and R anyhow." She stood up, uncomfortable with talking about herself. "It looks as if you're going to survive your spell, so I really do have to leave now."

Cass immediately unfolded his body to its full height and stepped forward. He brushed tendrils of flaming hair back with his fingers, and then touched soft, warm lips to her forehead. "Thanks for everything."

She gazed up into his face, her lips parted. The sensation of his kiss had spread through her whole body, hinting at a level of pleasure and excitement she had never experienced before. Apprehensive suddenly, she moved away and walked to the door, then glanced wistfully back at him. "Bye, Cass."

"Bye, Stormy," he said, an incomprehensible expression on his face. "See you around town."

Gayle walked quickly out to the car, thrown off balance by his offhand acquiescence to her leaving. She'd grown accustomed to his high-powered pressure to keep her there. "Well, good, I'm glad he gave in without a fight," she whispered. The last thing she needed was a hopeless entanglement.

But if she was so glad, why did she feel hurt instead of relieved? Climbing into her car, she answered aloud. "The sooner you forget all about Cass Starbaugh, the better."

Three

Gayle didn't see Cass again after they parted; but almost everyone in the small town had heard she'd been his nurse, however briefly, and seemed to feel obligated to report on his progress and activities.

After a week she went into the plumbing store to order budget bathroom fixtures, and the man behind the counter informed her that Cass was driving again and had come around to chat. "Looked good— you must've taken real fine care of him."

Even old Harvey Fenster had a word or two to say about him on her next visit. "I hope it pleases you to know Cass reamed me out for giving you a hard time. He says I need a tornado like you to shape me up. But I just want you to know that I'm not sure I agree with that. So you keep your distance until I make up my mind."

"Okay." Gayle stopped a few feet away from his bed. She knew it was difficult for so independent an old rancher to let go of the last shreds of control over his life.

He studied her, his eighty-year-old eyes cloudy

under shaggy white brows. "You don't look so special. How'd you hep Cass up like that?"

Good question, she thought, smiling wryly. "It wasn't me that hepped him up, it's you. You don't take proper care of yourself, and he's as worried about you as I am."

"I suppose he might be, at that—that's the kind of fellow he is," Harvey said, spacing his sentences around shortness of breath from his heart condition. "The year my wife died, he decided all on his own to come out and stay with me that first summer so I wouldn't have to be alone. Couldn't have been more than sixteen or so."

"Cass did that?" Gayle lifted her brows, surprised that a man who seemed so frivolous had done something so sensitive. She couldn't resist pumping Harvey a little. "I understand you're his great-uncle. . . . I've never known anyone who had so many relatives as Cass does. To hear him talk, he must be related to everyone in town."

He waved his hand. "Nah, he ain't got no blood kin whatsoever."

"Oh? Then why . . . ?"

"I ain't a gossip, if you want to know, ask Cass." He clamped his mouth shut and rested for a moment, catching his breath.

Gayle took advantage of his period of silence to examine him. When she finished and was packing her things away, Harvey said offhandedly, "I don't want to get in bad with Cass, so I suppose you can come around and be my nurse if you think you have to. But you better never mention nursing homes again. Got that?"

"Got it. How would it be if I arrange for personal-care attendants to come in and help with your cooking and care?"

"Is it gonna cost me?"

"Not as much as a nursing home."

"Well, all right then."

A few days later Gayle stopped at the paint store. The woman who shook her paint cans happily let drop that Cass had been seen with the Breckenridge girl again. Most people in town thought she was a front-runner in the roundup. Luckily, by that time Gayle had developed a talent for smiling and nodding noncommittally to any news about him.

At the hardware store the fellow behind the counter advised her, "Every builder in the whole damn county danced a jig when Cass's doctor gave him the okay to do a light job or two with his heavy equipment. That means he'll be in shape when the building season starts. He's the only man with a backhoe and dozer if you want any diggin' done, yessir."

After three weeks had passed, Gayle went into the Coffee Cup, one of the more popular restaurants in town, to treat herself to lunch between patients. She stopped short just inside the door when she saw the man himself holding court in a back booth. He looked hale and hearty, with his arm free of the sling and his long legs stretched out in the aisle. Three young women were sitting with him, and a couple more were standing around giggling at his patter.

She didn't wait to find out if one of them was the Breckenridge girl. Backing out before he saw her, she went to another restaurant and sat rigidly erect, sipping coffee, appalled by how jealous she felt.

On Saturday Gayle got up and breakfasted early, then put on her remodeling outfit and a pair of leather gloves. She knew she'd have to pay a plumber to install her new bathroom fixtures. But her finances were critically short, so she hoped to save a few dollars by removing the old fixtures and wall tiles herself. The tiles came down easily enough, but she could only mutter in frustration over a pipe wrench, when she tried to take out the sink.

Suddenly, a rumble shook the house. "Earthquake!" she cried, conditioned to living on the Pacific Coast.

But it wasn't an earthquake: There were engine sounds behind the rumble and vibration. Running into the bedroom, she looked out the window. "Oh, my gosh!" she said.

The bed of an enormous dump truck was rising into the air. The last of a dozen easy-chair-size boulders was sliding out, and boulders were rolling in every direction over her side yard. Someone must have delivered them to the wrong place.

Pipe wrench forgotten in her hand, Gayle ran out the front door and dashed around the side of the house. By the time she'd stumbled through a two-foot-tall jungle of dead knapweeds, she'd begun to suspect the delivery wasn't a mistake, and that it meant trouble. The truckbed was being lowered , and the logo on the door was J&C Excavating. The face grinning at her from the window was Cass's, his red cap sitting jauntily atop his sandy hair.

A spurt of irrational joy hit her. She ran a hand over her rebellious curls, but a brisk, spring-scented breeze immediately whipped them into a tangle again. She wished she'd put more effort into her makeup, and that she was dressed in anything other than her tattered jeans and a sweatshirt stiff with dried paint spatters. Reining in her wayward thoughts, she clicked her tongue with annoyance. "What difference does it make how I look?"

When the truck bed was horizontal, Cass turned off the engine and jumped down out of the cab as agiley as if he'd never suffered a life-threatening injury. "Well, hello there, Stormy—long time no see," he drawled. "How're you doing?"

"I . . . I . . ." The sight of the boulders filling her yard was numbing, but the sight of Cass walking toward her in jeans well worn enough to cling to the contours of his long, muscular legs struck her mute. His shoulders looked impossibly wide under a torso-fitting yellow western shirt.

He slapped the biggest boulder, tall as his waist. "These are some rocks, aren't they? Best of the lot I brought out of the mountains the other day. Nice healthy moss on 'em."

She stared at him for a moment, then at the boulders. Tucking the eighteen-inch wrench under one arm, she waved her leather-gloved hand toward the original shambles of her yard. "Didn't I have problems enough to begin with? Why did you *do* this?"

His grin turned smug, and he tucked his fingers into his jeans' rear pockets. "These are for your rock garden. We talked about it the first day we met."

"We did not talk about any such thing!"

"Yes, we did. You said I'd love doing your yard."

"No!" An inkling of memory came back. "Well, yes, maybe I said that, but I was just making conversation. *You* were the one who mentioned rock gardens, not me. *I* have no intention of doing anything more than killing the weeds and maybe straightening out the ground with a rake. Why on earth didn't you ask me before you brought this mountain of rocks?"

Cass waved off her protest. "I figured you'd trust me, because I drove by your place a few times until I finally understood your yard problems." He pointed at a pile of dirt, overgrown with new green shoots. "That must be the topsoil they skinned off when they dug the basement—how long ago? The house must be ten, fifteen years old. They didn't spread it back, they didn't even backfill. I'm surprised your basement isn't flooded, with that moat of melting snow around the house."

He grinned happily at her, his brown eyes twinkling. "Nobody would buy a house with such a genuine disaster area of a yard, Stormy."

"But . . . but . . ." Her heart sank over the magnitude of her problems.

"Let me explain what I think you should do." Cass walked across the yard to look down the hill behind the house. At the back edge of her property was a small stream, and beyond that two beef cattle and a herd of horses were grazing in a field. "If you kill the knapweeds and leave the backyard natural with wild grass and flowers, you might have bitterroots blooming in May."

"Natural." Gayle brightened as she stood beside him. "Now that sounds like something I can afford."

He turned and looked at the house. "But you'll want to build up the hill with a few boulders where it slopes away, and put some trees in around the house." His Montana drawl had disappeared in his enthusiasm. Frowning, he paced off the overly long side yard to the end. "You should build a mound out here with the rest of the rocks, and plant it with flowers and shrubs. And sod in a sculptured lawn."

Gayle followed two steps behind him, becoming more worried by the minute. Natural and economical had been left behind on the hill.

Cass's drawl came back as he finished his spiel. "Yes, ma'am, Stormy, this place is gonna look like something right out of *House Beautiful*. Mmm-hmmm."

"*House Beautiful!*" she whispered, clutching the wrench in both hands. "But how am I supposed to do all the things you're talking about? It sounds like an enormous job."

"Never you worry, Jackson's on his way over with the backhoe. I'll get the yard shaped up and leveled out, then place these babies." He patted the tallest boulder, which probably weighed a ton.

"The *backhoe*!" She pushed her blazing hair off her forehead and glanced at the dump truck, trying to guess what he must charge by the hour. "Listen, I don't know where you got the idea that I wanted landscaping. But you'd better get this straight, right up front—I simply do not have any money to pay for your backhoe, or your labor, or your rocks . . . or any of this."

He lifted his shoulders and held out his hands, palms up. "No charge."

Gayle sat abruptly down on a boulder and stared up at him. "Are you saying you'd do all that work for *free*?"

He scratched his head, settled his cap, and glanced impishly out from under the bill. "No-o-o, not for free exactly. I'll expect a little something in return."

She crossed her legs, her knee sticking out through the stringy hole in her jeans, and looked him up and down. "And what, exactly, are you expecting as payment?"

A teasing "gotcha" gleam lit his eyes. "Why, Miz Stromm, I'm shocked that you'd suspect such a thing of me," he said, exaggerating his drawl. "I never buy *that*! When we get around to doing what you're thinking, it'll be out of mutual consent." He let his sultry gaze rove down over her tall shape, her curves evident despite her baggy clothes.

Her face went hot as desire burst to life in the secret corners of her body. "Don't talk to me like that!" she snapped, irritated at herself for responding to his

playful little seduction. "What exactly *are* you thinking of asking in payment?"

"Going back to the first day we met, you had a few
very opinionated things to say about my mountain
climbing." His smile disappeared, and his brown
eyes narrowed, as if he was covering some emotion.
"All I want in return for my services is the opportunity to introduce you to my mountains, and maybe
prove I'm not the harebrained idiot you seem to think
I am."

She balanced the wrench on her crossed knees and
stared at him, her chin thrust forward, her mouth
ajar. "You mean my company is all you want? You
really do go to extremes to defend your ego, don't
you?"

Cass propped a lean hip on top of the largest
boulder. "Mmm, I suppose ego might have something
to do with it."

Gayle studied him curiously. "What earthly difference does it make what I think?"

He shrugged his shoulders, pulling the fitted yellow shirt even closer around his chest. "I sure as hell
don't know, but it does seem to."

"Thanks a lot," she said wryly. "But if you think I'm
going to claw my way up a cliff so you can make
points for your pride, then you might just as well pick
up your rocks and cart them away again."

"Now, *that'd* cost you," he said, crossing the arms.
His sleeves were rolled up over his biceps, and the
springy hairs on his forearms shone gold in the
sunlight. "If you can't bring yourself to let me fix your
yard in exchange for a little of your time, then you'll
have to hire me to tote the rubble away."

"Cass Starbaugh, that's *blackmail*."

"Yea-ah," he said, a grin lighting his face. "But
forget the climbing, I'm not ready for that myself yet."
He patted the top of his boulder. "These are just my

little way of asking if you'd like to go on a picnic with me tomorrow."

"A picnic?" she repeated. "Are you by any chance asking me out on a date, or something like that?"

"Something like that," he admitted sheepishly. "Why not?"

"No reason, I guess. It's just a surprise, after I haven't heard a word from you for almost a month. What made you think of me all of a sudden?"

"Oh, I've been thinking about you all along. I suppose I didn't want to see you again until I got back in top shape." He gave a wry smile. "Ego again."

A thrill leaped in her chest, but she shot it down quickly with a bit of gossip she'd heard. "I thought you and—who was it?—that Breckenridge girl were a couple. I don't feel any particular inclination to enter into a competition for you."

Cass had the grace to look embarrassed. "How'd you hear about her?"

She rested her elbow on the wrench. "Several people mentioned that she's your steady date."

"That's just small-town speculation. Maybe I've gone around with her a few times, but no promises have been made, not even any maybes. She's like a cousin to me, sort of. Or a sister."

Gayle studied his face, wondering what his "sort of" relatives were all about. "Well, I don't know, I still think this yard-and-rock business is a little bizarre. Why didn't you just pick up the phone and ask me if I'd go on a picnic with you?"

"What fun would that have been? The expression on your face when you came running out was worth the effort." He laughed and settled himself more comfortably, pulling one knee up with his boot sole wedged against the side of the rock.

Gayle jerked her gaze away from the pull of his jeans around his thigh and pelvis. "That's all that's important to you, isn't it? Fun and joking and teasing."

"What else makes life worth living?" he countered, grinning down at her. "Tell me, Stormy, how long has it been since you took a day off to have fun and laugh?"

"Don't call me Stormy! And I'll take plenty of days off when I finally get this house remodeled and sold."

"In other words, you haven't taken any time off, have you? Come on, Ms. Stromm, say yes, go on that picnic with me tomorrow."

She could feel him wearing her down, and flung her two gloved hands out in exasperation. The wrench fell off her crossed knees and thudded on the ground. "Why me?"

"Because you're a challenge, and I do dearly love a challenge."

"I might have guessed." Gayle sighed, realizing that by so cautiously holding him at arm's length, she'd actually piqued his interest. At least now she knew exactly where she stood. He'd lose interest quickly enough if she gave in to him.

"Come on, Stormy, take a chance, say yes."

"It's tempting, I'll admit," she said, his lighthearted game-playing beginning to soften her. She looked at the mountains. The warmth of mid-April had pushed the snowline up so high, only the rugged peaks were white, like a child's exaggerated drawing. Then she shook her head and picked up the heavy pipe wrench. "But I really can't spare the time. It'll take me all weekend to wrestle the old fixtures out of my bathroom."

Cass reached out and took the wrench out of her hand. "Phew, it's a relief to hear you're working on a bathroom. I thought you brought this thing out to bash over my head,"

"I probably should have," she said, laughing.

He got up, swinging the wrench like a baseball bat a couple of times. "Maybe I can speed up your bathroom project. Then would you picnic with me?"

"Don't tell me you're a plumber too." She stood up and brushed off the seat of her jeans.

"I'm a pretty good excavator, but I don't do toilets," he said in a deadpan tone. "However, I do know a plumber who owes me. I'll call in my chit and have him do the job for you for free. Mind if I use your phone?"

Without waiting for an answer, he started across the yard, swinging the wrench at dead knapweeds.

"Cass, wait!" Gayle cried out, still vacillating. She started after him, but stopped short and stared when a flatbed truck pulled up at the side of the road. The big yellow backhoe was piggybacked on it. A good-looking dark-haired man got out of the cab and began undoing one of the enormous chains holding it down.

She strode purposefully forward. "I expect you must be Jackson."

He gave her a nod and a sweet, shy smile, then dropped the first chain with a crash and went on to the next.

"Wait a minute!" Gayle said. "I haven't said I want this backhoe yet—or those rocks, for that matter."

Jackson glanced at her, then at the house into which Cass had disappeared; a spark of speculative amusement in his eyes. Lifting his shoulders in a shrug, he dropped the second chain.

When it became obvious she wasn't getting through to him, Gayle sat down on the boulder and blew out a frustrated, bewildered breath. Within minutes he'd unloaded the backhoe and driven the dump truck away. Cass came out of the house and climbed into the backhoe, firing up the engine.

Within an hour a plumber and his helper arrived.

Somewhere along the way Gayle had completely lost control of the situation. For the rest of the day all she could do was stand aside and let things happen.

The sun was sinking behind the mountains and the plumber was long gone when Cass finally drove the backhoe up onto the flatbed and chained it down. Dusting his hands, he said, "Okay, that's that. I sure as hell hope you can't think of any other excuses for not going on that picnic tomorrow."

"How could I, when you've been so incredibly helpful?" She turned in a circle, arms wrapped around her body, looking over the yard. "I'm utterly overwhelmed."

"Good, I intend to see that you stay that way, Stormy."

"Stop calling me Stormy," she said, for lack of a better comeback.

He grinned and cocked a finger at her.

Watching him hop up into the cab of the truck, she began to wonder somewhat belatedly exactly what she had committed herself to. Cass Starbaugh had proved today, as if he hadn't already, that he was way above her league in not only experience, but craftiness and persistence.

Four

Cass went to church early on Sunday morning, and by eleven o'clock he was on his way across the valley. The sense of elation he felt over seeing Gayle again had him floating two inches off the ground—or at this point, off the seat of his spanking clean pickup, washed, waxed, and polished up for the occasion.

He'd hoped staying away from her for a month and seeing other women would cure him of his attraction, but he still felt like a damned, obsessed adolescent with stars in his eyes. Since separation didn't help, he was hoping a little intensive togetherness, such as a picnic on his own home turf, would cure him of his crush.

Parking on the potholed driveway outside her house, Cass ran up the steps of the rickety porch to knock on the door. Waiting, he dusted his cowboy boots against the backs of his legs, jerked his denim jacket straight, smoothed his hair, and rubbed his palms over his jaw to be sure he hadn't missed any spots shaving.

A few seconds later Gayle opened the door and looked up at him with those unsettling light gray eyes. "Well, hello, Mr. Starbaugh," she said, sending a little tremor through him with her husky voice. "You're right on time to the dot."

"And hello there, Miz Stromm. I'm always on time when there's something worth rushing to." He looked her over, an answering grin creeping appreciatively over his face. Her beige corduroy pants fit her long legs and rounded hips like a second skin, and her navy-blue blouse looked soft and new. She had her hair pulled back in a ponytail.

Cass's grin faltered when he noticed that she looked tired and tense, with dark smudges under her eyes. He hoped she wasn't upset over his blackmailing her into spending time with him. If she'd put up any kind of serious protest, he would have picked up his rocks and dropped issue. "How about you?" he asked cautiously. "If you're not ready and raring to go, this is your last chance to back out."

"Oh, I'm not going to back out." She slipped her arms into the sleeves of a white sweater and flipped her ponytail free in back. "But I'll reserve judgment about the raring part. After skyrockets and boulders, I'm almost afraid to imagine what you might come up with next."

Cass put on an innocent face. "Nothing, I'm on my best behavior today."

"I'm not sure what best behavior means in your case."

"It means I promise not to call you Stormy all day."

"In that case let's do this picnic thing," she said with a laugh.

When she brushed past him to step out onto the porch, the slight contact brought his body to attention. His fingers fairly twitched to touch her, leading him to suspect intensive togetherness wasn't going to be the solution to his crush.

Blodgett Canyon was only five bumpy miles west of

town. Gayle was quiet, offering no conversation, so Cass, a nervous talker, filled the silence with chatter about the small ranches they were passing. Each one was rich in local history and inhabited by a "sort of" relative. He could feel her studying his face intently while he talked, apparently not very interested in the landmarks he pointed out. After fifteen minutes he was tired of listening to himself too.

He abruptly fell silent when he caught a glimpse of the hundred-foot cliffs rising straight up out of the narrow canyon. It was his first time back since the accident, and his reaction was so strong, he might have turned tail and run if Gayle hadn't been sitting beside him. He'd rather die of an anxiety attack than have her guess he was afraid.

He decided if he didn't desensitize his phobia, he'd never climb again, and picnicking in the shadow of the cliffs was as good a form of shock therapy as any.

Swinging into the parking area by the picnic ground, Cass turned off the engine and came around to hand Gayle down out of the pickup. The air was filled with a piny scent from the forest and a roar from the stream, which was swollen by the spring runoff. "This has always been one of my favorite places," he said, fixing his gaze on her face, letting her peer up at the cliffs on her own. "What do you think of them?"

She glanced at him. "I think they're awesome, that's what I think. I feel like they're bending in, ready to fall on me."

"Would you rather go somewhere else?" he asked, hoping for a face-saving excuse to back out of a tricky situation.

But she smiled and said, "Of course not. I'm here so you can teach me to like them, remember? So start teaching."

"Mmm-hmmm," Cass said with a sigh. He slipped a backpack over his shoulders, and lifted a large cooler out of the bed of the pickup. He glanced at the people scattered all around the campground and picnic area. "I know a perfect place away from everyone, but I'm not sure how much walking you're up to."

She held out a foot. "I've got my handy-dandy hiking boots on."

"Well, so you have. You keep surprising me. The way you talked about the mountains, I got the impression you weren't an outdoorsy kind of girl."

There was a teasing tone in her laugh. "It may also surprise you to hear that mountains aren't the only kind of outdoors there is. It just so happens that back home in Portland, I love to hike on the coast and along the Columbia River."

"Interesting," he murmured, fitting another piece into the puzzle of Gayle.

The trail began at a U.S. Forest Service sign marking the boundary of a wilderness area. From there it ran up the left-hand side of the canyon, at the base of gently rounded hills. The cliffs were on the right side, semihidden by trees. In the branches Chickadees whistled and squirrels chirred protests at the trespassers.

Cass kept the better part of his attention fixed on Gayle, fascinated by the way her body moved under the tight cords. But he couldn't tell if she was enjoying the walk or not; she was the damndest woman for concealing her thoughts behind those freckles of hers.

Her silence spurred him into expounding upon the geological formation of the cliffs, and thoroughly boring himself. He was only too happy to finally walk off the trail and say, "This is it. Think you can eat a picnic lunch here?"

Gayle walked out onto the flat stone formation. It was surrounded by budding aspens and graceful pines, with a backdrop of the granite cliffs and the sunny blue sky. The same scene was perfectly reflected in a placid, crystal-clear pool. A breeze that smelled as crisp and intoxicating as champagne lifted her hair. "Oh, Cass, it's absolutely beautiful. So perfectly peaceful."

"Yea-ah." Impossibly pleased by her reaction, he put the cooler down and spread a blanket from the backpack over the rock. "There you go, Miz Stromm. This is your day off, all you have to do is settle back and enjoy."

"I think I can cope with that," Gayle said, taking off her sweater. Her dark blue blouse made her skin look as delicate as creamy satin. She lowered herself gracefully to the blanket and folded her long, shapely legs Indian-style.

Keeping half an eye on that tempting view, Cass went down on his knees to unpack a pale green tablecloth to spread on the stone slab, setting china plates, silver, and linen napkins for two. Opening the cooler, he took out a pink rose in a bud vase and two candles to put in the center of the cloth. He struck several matches, muttering under his breath when the candles wouldn't stay lit.

"I don't believe this," she exclaimed, laughing softly. "I'm overwhelmed again!"

"That's the name of the game." He gave up on the candles and took plastic containers of potato salad, coleslaw, and cold chicken out of the cooler, and a round loaf of French bread on a board. "And the *pièce de résistance*," he said, holding up a bottle and two wineglasses. "This is the damned wine you've been refusing to share with me. Try and wiggle out of it now."

"I'm too flabbergasted to try!" She gave an amazed laugh and accepted the glass of white wine.

"Here's to the mountains," Cass murmured, his

back solidly turned toward the cliffs, and lifted his glass.

"To the mountains—which I'm rapidly coming to appreciate." She clinked her glass against his and sipped. "You certainly have a talent for doing things up right, don't you?"

He grinned. "Admit it—you think I'm a total idiot."

"No, I don't!" She bent forward and laid her hand on his arm. "I'm incredibly impressed by all the effort you've put into this picnic. It's so . . . romantic." The instant she said it, she jerked her hand away from his arm, her face going pink. "I mean nice. It's *nice*."

A smile crept across Cass's lips when he realized a chink was opening up in her armor. "Romantic is a perfectly legitimate word." He tapped the bottle and the bread, then leaned forward to cup his palm around her cheek. Her skin was baby-soft. A current of electricity even stronger tnan the one he'd felt the first day crackled between them. His voice was husky as he said, "Old Omar the poet said romance is a jug of wine, a loaf of bread—and thou, beside me singing in the wilderness . . . just like us, here."

Her lips parted as she gazed into his eyes with an almost shocked look. Jerking away from his hand, she smiled, went sober, smiled again, then tried to pretend she hadn't felt the electricity too. "All right, this *is* romantic. I can't think of any other word to describe what you've done to me—I mean to *here*. I mean the picnic."

His smile stretched into a teasing grin. "Oh, go ahead and admit it, you're attracted to me, aren't you? If you do, I'll admit to spending some restless nights over you too. What's wrong with facing up to that? It's human nature."

Now that it was out in the open, Gayle relaxed and

laughed. "I refuse to admit to anything, and don't you get any ideas."

Cass made a show of brushing down his blue denim jacket and jeans. "Do I look like an idea kind of guy?"

"You look like ideas personified, and you know it!" Laughing, she ran her fingers up into the hair tumbling over her forehead. "And as for Omar the poet, it'd be deadly if you expect me to sing."

He caressed her face with his gaze. "Singing isn't necessary, just give me thou in the wilderness, and I'll be happy. What would it take to make you happy?"

Gayle's smoky-gray eyes were soft as her gaze touched skittishly on his lips, his shoulders, his chest. Sighing, she turned to look around the little woodsy bower. "I truthfully can't remember ever being happier than I am right now." Retreating from the light sensuality they'd brushed into, she nodded at the plastic containers on the tablecloth. "I'm starving. Are you going to open those, or are they just for looks?"

"Good idea." He put down his glass and began dishing up food. "Then you don't regret my bullying you into coming here with me?"

She took her plate and shook her head. "No, I'm glad you did. I enjoy being here with you, probably lots more than is good for me."

"Well, I'm certainly glad to hear that." Cass sat down with his back against a tree trunk and stretched his legs out. "You've been so quiet, I couldn't tell."

"I'm quiet because I'm tired, I guess," she said, holding her plate on her lap. "I didn't get much sleep last night."

He forked up a few hungry bites of food, studying the smudges under her eyes. "I hope you weren't so upset about my boulders that it gave you insomnia."

She shook her head. "No, I got used to them as

soon as you arranged them so nicely. I couldn't sleep because I had bad dreams, and not about you."

"Of course not—you wouldn't catch me starring in a nightmare." He pointed his fork at her. "When I come sneaking in on you while you're asleep, it'll be a different kind of dream altogether."

"Honestly, Cass, you'd better do something about that ego of yours." Her eyes danced as she finished the wine in her glass.

"That's not ego, just the facts, ma'am." He refilled her glass and pointed at her plate. "Eat your food before you get tipsy."

Unfolding her legs, Gayle moved closer to Cass, using a neighboring tree trunk for a backrest. She put her plate in her lap again and began eating. He found himself fascinated by the seductive motion of her lips in chewing. Crossing his legs the other way, he ended up thigh to thigh with her, and hoped it was significant that she didn't move away.

They ate in companionable silence for a few minutes, and then she pointed a bitten drumstick at him. "Everything is delicious. Did you cook this?"

He shook his head. "Hilda fixed the food for me."

She aimed a scowl at him. "Hilda, my boss? She'd love to see me involved in a nice sticky local affair, to keep me in Home Health. Should I get the feeling that people are ganging up on me?"

He laughed. "Not at all, see she's—"

"I know, I know," she broke in, "she's 'sort of' your aunt. What are these 'sort of' relatives of yours anyway?"

"If you're a good girl, I'll explain it to you someday," he answered lightly, as defensive about his personal history as he was about the cliffs. "Now eat your food and quit complaining."

When she'd finished eating, Gayle rinsed her plate off in the pool, then stretched out on her back on the blanket, sighing deeply. "I'm utterly replete."

After rolling his jacket up to tuck under her head, Cass lay down on his stomach, braced up on his elbows to look into her face. He asked the question he'd wanted to earlier. "What were your nightmares about?"

"Blood and gore." She grimaced and looked up into the gently waving pine branches, a frown creasing her forehead. "They stem from a little burnout problem I have."

"Burned out on what?"

She looked at him for a moment, then apparently decided to answer. "Critical Care—specifically on trauma patients. Car accidents, gunshot wounds, domestic abuse, you name it. Ordinary profoundly ill people didn't seem to bother me, but I couldn't be objective about all that blood and pain. When I started dreaming about mangled bodies every night, my supervisor made me take a leave of absence. I can't go back until I quit dreaming and get things back into perspective."

Cass studied her with surprise, fitting in an unexpected puzzle piece. "It never occurred to me you had a major crisis going on in your life. Your take-charge, Miz Professional act must be Academy Award material."

Her eyes flashed anger. She sat up and wrapped her arms around her knees. "It's no act! I'm damned good at what I do. I liked working in Critical Care a lot. It may be stressful, but it's also exciting and rewarding. I didn't want to give it up, and I have every intention of going back to it again."

"Home Health is important too," Cass said for the sake of argument.

"I know it is!" she said impatiently. "Oh, how can I explain? Being a Critical Care nurse is like being a fighter pilot, while working for Home Health is being a flight attendant."

"Mmm-*hmmm*." Cass sat up, too, and grinned at

her. "Could it be I'm not the only one troubled with pride and ego?"

She grinned back. "I'll admit it's a job that requires a good, healthy ego. Maybe that's my problem, I'm not cocksure enough of myself. Anyhow, I'm still dreaming about mangled bodies—every time I went to sleep last night. Finally, I couldn't face them any longer, so I got up and painted another wall instead."

"Why the devil didn't you tell me you were exhausted, instead of letting me drag you to hell and gone? We could have picnicked ten feet from the pickup."

She smiled. "I'm glad we didn't. The peace of this place is rubbing off on me."

"I'm happy to hear that."

Turning her head, Gayle looked toward the right side of the canyon for several minutes. "That's where you had your accident, isn't it? On those cliffs."

Cass started. He'd been so fascinated by her presence that he'd forgotten the cliffs were there, behind his back. He lifted his cap and ran his fingers through his hair, then cleared his throat. "That's the place, I'm afraid."

"Did you bring me here thinking the beauty would convince me mountain climbing is safe and tame?"

"Not really. Well, maybe—sort of," he admitted, though it had been himself he'd hoped to convince: a notion that now seemed one of his more serious mental lapses. "But if I did, it was because I didn't know about your burnout problem and why you feel the way you do about my climbing. Why don't we just forget it and talk about something else?"

"No, I don't want to forget it. If I'm going to be around you, I need to understand," she said, continuing to study him with narrowed eyes. "Where did it happen, exactly? How?"

He blew out a reluctant breath and turned, coming up on one knee. He stared at the cliff, a prickle of cold sweat breaking out on his face. It took a moment before he was able to speak. "Look between those two trees, over there to your left. See that pinnacle, maybe twenty feet up from the rubble at the base of the cliff?"

"There must be a dozen pinnacles. Which one?"

Swinging around, Cass knelt on both knees behind her. Taking her head between his two hands, he tilted it to the proper angle. It surprised him that the simple physical contact soothed his anxiety somewhat. "The one with the patch of lighter color above it."

"Oh, there—yes."

Now that Gayle had the place spotted, he didn't have to look any longer. He gazed instead down into the sweetly scented tangle of copper curls on her head. "My accident came about when a big slab of rock broke off up there, and I got caught in the avalanche."

Her body went rigid, a bare inch away from his. "The cliff is beautiful, I guess, but it looks so dangerous. I just can't imagine why anyone would want to climb it."

Cass put his arms around her shoulders to comfort and reassure her—or himself—and clasped his hands loosely in front of her. "Actually, not even an expert climber should climb there. It's obviously too fragile."

"But obviously one did." She thought for a moment. "Do you usually climb in February? That's when you got hurt, wasn't it?"

He fervently wished they could leave the subject behind, but it didn't appear she'd be satisfied until she knew the whole story. "No, most people wouldn't climb in February, but a bunch of high school boys came out here for a party, and they did."

"A party in the winter? Wasn't it ten feet high with snow?"

Cass shook his head. "The climate in the valley is

mild for Montana, and there'd been a February thaw. Anyhow, the boys came out with a keg of beer. The beer replaced their common sense with false courage, and they decided to climb the cliff. One of them found out that going up wasn't so difficult, but coming back down was. He got stuck, and Search and Rescue was called to get him out of his predicament."

Gayle's head snapped around again, and she peered into his face, only inches away. "Search and Rescue?"

"We're a team trained for mountain rescue—finding lost people and locating plane crashes in inaccessible places, that sort of thing. Not to mention climbing cliffs to bring down stranded kids. I almost had him down when half a wall of rock broke loose. Sounded like a barrage of artillery."

She clasped his hands in hers. "I know what happened to you, but did the boy get hurt?"

"Luckily, he happened to end up under my body, so he came out with only a few bruises and scratches."

"I see," Gayle said, as if she'd guessed much more than his words had told. Relaxing her rigid spine, she leaned back against his chest. Her delicate flowery perfume wafted around him. "I'll have to rethink my first impressions of you."

He laughed softly and crossed his arms around her body, cuddling her close. It seemed so natural, as if he'd been waiting all his life to hold her. "There's a lot more to you than I first thought too. It appears we're just a couple of fighter pilots trying to save civilization from a hostile world."

"It seems so, doesn't it? We're both hazardous to our own health."

"That's true enough."

As Cass held her, he forgot all about the cliff. Instead he became very aware of her breasts pressed against his arms, of the lushness of her body curved into his. A very independent part of him stirred to life. And what had begun as taking and giving comfort turned into something else entirely.

Putting his hands under Gayle's elbows, he lifted her to her knees, and turned her to face him. Just as he had imagined the first time he saw her, he discovered this tall, full-bodied woman filled the arms of a big man like himself just fine—mmm-hmmm.

Smiling down at her, Cass gazed at the shape of her nose and chin, caressed the roundness of her cheeks. It occurred to him suddenly that her riotous freckles were the most cunning beauty marks he'd ever seen. Lowering his head, he tried to kiss each one. She gave a quick little gasp when he touched his lips to hers, nibbling, testing. But she didn't push him away.

Covering her mouth, he eagerly savored her female taste and softness. Her breath warmed his cheek in quick, erratic little puffs. Her hands moved up over his chest, leaving a trail of fire, until she'd curled her arms around his neck, pulling him closer.

She shivered when he ran his tongue slowly from one corner of her mouth to the other, teasing for entry. When her lips parted, he entered paradise and probed her mouth with his tongue. He'd never experienced anything like the electrical chemistry tingling between them. Cupping his hands around her buttocks, he pressed her pelvis to his body, pushing his knee between her legs. Then, supporting her with his arms, he lowered her down onto the blanket.

But the instant her back touched ground, Gayle stiffened and jerked away from him as if she'd suddenly come to her senses. "Cass, no," she whispered. "We can't. . . . I don't want this."

He lifted his head and looked down into her flushed face and molten eyes. "Yes, you do, honey."

"No! Yes . . . maybe . . . but . . ." She rolled away

from him and sat up, rubbing her face. "No, I don't! Not here!"

He twisted around and sat up beside her, taking her hands in his. "Where, sweetheart?"

"Nowhere!" Jerking her hands away as if he'd burned her, she leaped to her feet and retreated from the blanket.

Cass gazed longingly up at her. "But *why*? You want me, too, I know you do."

Gayle pressed a hand to either side of her face, and glanced yearningly, he thought, at his shoulders, his chest, even touched upon the painful condition of his lower body. "We'd be great together," he said, picking up his siege. "Fireworks like you've never seen yet."

Her eyes narrowed. "I don't remember anything about fireworks being mentioned in the boulder/picnic agreement."

"Not specifically, I suppose, but . . ." He looked mournfully down at himself. "What do you suggest I do about this?"

She stared at him for a moment, then reached down into the pool and splashed a handful of icy water at him. "Maybe a little swim would take care of it."

Cass shot one long arm out toward her ankle. "You're asking for it, Stormy."

She skipped out of reach. "Tell you what, you nurse your condition, and I'll pack away the remains of our picnic. How would that be?"

"I'd rather have you nurse it," he grumbled, but all he got in reply was a snort.

Within an hour they were back on Gayle's porch. "When can I see you again?" Cass asked, pushing his hands into his jeans pockets.

"Don't even think about it," she said regretfully. "I'm only going to be here another month or so. It would cause all sorts of complications if we got involved."

"Who said anything about getting involved? I just want to *see* you again, have some laughs."

She put a palm on either side of his face. "After what happened this afternoon, do you honestly think we could just *see* each other, Starbaugh?"

He put his palms over her hands and gave a crooked smile. "You can't blame me for trying, can you?"

"I would have been disappointed if you hadn't." She went up on her toes to brush a kiss on his lips. "Thanks for the picnic. The day has been fun and very interesting." She paused a beat to smile. "All of it."

Cass felt bereft when she went inside. He stared at the closed door, tempted to knock and bring her back. He even lifted his fist, but dropped it again when he realized she was right. Whatever was going on between them was too strong to take lightly. It smacked of permanent commitment, and that was as scary to him as the cliff.

As he walked toward his pickup, he was certain about only one thing. His plan to neutralize his crush had backfired royally.

Gayle watched Cass walk toward the street. Everything, from the way the breeze lifted his sun-streaked hair down to the way his knees canted out to the sides when he walked, seemed cunning enough to wrench her heart.

When he reached his pickup, he looked back and saw her. His grin and wave caused her entire body, inside and out, to respond all over again, as it had to his kiss. Fighting an urge to call him back into the house, she managed a good-bye wave.

After he'd driven away, she felt lonelier than she'd ever felt in her life. Wandering restlessly through her little house, she stopped in front of the living-room window. Though she was gazing down at the huge pile of dead knapweeds Cass had bulldozed into the back corner of her yard, she was actually seeing a replay of their last four hours together. Hearing the sound of his voice. Feeling his tall, husky body against hers again.

Another image superimposed itself like a double exposure over the other—Cass climbing the cliff, rocks crashing down on him. His mangled body. "No!" she cried out, splaying her hands across her face.

Taking an impatient breath to collect herself, she stomped across the house to the bedroom. It was ridiculous for a woman like her to be mooning over a man like Cass. Okay, so he wasn't the playboy she'd first thought. Maybe they were both fighter pilots, but that didn't mean they were suited for each other. She'd been a fool to let herself become so . . . affected by him.

"'Affected'!" jeered a little voice in her mind. "Why don't you tell it like it is? You're falling in—"

"*I am not!*" she exclaimed, stripping off her woodsy-smelling, Cass-scented clothes.

"Well, a little, maybe. But once I'm back home in Portland, things will go back to normal," she vowed.

Five

"Where *are* you, Gayle?"

She jumped when Hilda touched her shoulder during a Home Health staff meeting. Glancing around, she realized with some confusion that the only staff members left in the conference room were herself and her boss. "Where is everybody?"

"You left us mentally about an hour ago, so you missed not only the last half of the meeting, but a relatively rambunctious nursing exodus as well. It isn't like you to go off into never-never land," said Hilda, studying her with concerned eyes. "What's going on?"

Gayle slumped down and ran her fingers through her hair. "I guess I've been preoccupied with something else." In the eight days since the picnic she'd had to contend with Cass lurking in the corners of her mind, ready to crowd out everything else if she let her guard down the slightest bit. Instead of feeling grateful, she felt hurt that he'd taken her at her word and not tried to see her again. It wasn't fair that he could shuck her out of his mind so easily, while she was trapped in a daze over him.

"You're doing it again!"

Gayle snapped back to the present, offering a lame "Sorry."

Hilda scowled over half-glasses. "How many times have you gone out and had fun in the month and a half since you've been here?"

"Well, once I guess." Once too many; it'd ruined her.

"Are you trying to burn yourself out on Home Health too?"

Gayle straightened up resentfully. "If you aren't happy with the way I'm doing my work, why don't you say so? Have my patients been complaining?"

"Of course not. Your patients consider you the best thing to hit the valley since Lewis and Clark trekked through. I'm not worried about your performance, I'm worried about you looking pale and drawn and tired. Have you made any friends in town?"

"I haven't had—" She broke off short of reinforcing Hilda's point.

"I want you to go out and meet some young, single people and have fun. Ask Cass to introduce you around. If anyone knows where the action is, he does."

"Cass! What made you think of him?"

"How could I not, when he's taken to visiting me here every day? By some odd happenstance our chats always come around to you."

"Me!" Gayle struggled to hide her elation. He'd been thinking about her after all!

"Yes, you. And I'm sure he'd be glad to introduce you around. If you're shy, I can give him a call and ask him."

"Don't you dare, or I'll quit on the spot!" Gayle jumped to her feet.

"Don't worry, I won't interfere. Here's another thought—you know that new beauty shop that just opened up? The owner used to do hair for a movie studio in California, and the young women have been hanging around, probably hoping she'll make them look like stars. Go over there and stir up some social life for yourself. I'm your boss, and that's an order."

"Oh, all right, I'll think about it." Gayle picked up her bag and retreated toward the door. "I've got to go, I'm due to see Harvey Fenster."

"How's that house of yours coming along?" Harvey asked, after telling a long tale of woe about running a ranch from his bed. Gayle was trying to listen to his heart with her stethoscope, but his gab made hearing virtually impossible.

She decided satisfying his hunger for the sound of a human voice would do him more good than keeping track of his failing body. "It's coming along pretty well. The kitchen is a disaster area yet, and I have to replace the carpets and linoleum."

"Heard you had some help with your yard."

She flinched. If even a bedridden old man knew, then everyone knew what had gone on between her and Cass. "I guess I did. Now I have to plant some grass and flowers. And find someone to cart away a mountain of dead knapweeds."

"Oh, hell, don't waste your money having that done. Everyone around here burns their knapweeds. Nothin' to it. Just splash some kerosene on 'em and light a match."

"Hmmm, that's an idea," Gayle said, packing her things away in her bag. "Do you have any problems I should know about before I leave?"

"Only that there's a ton of work I should be takin' care of on the ranch. And don't you be sayin' I'll be on my feet and back at it in no time." Harvey rubbed the wispy white hair on his head and breathed oxygen through a mask for a few seconds. "I've got brains enough to know I've bought the ticket."

There wasn't much Gayle could say to that, so she sat down beside his bed to offer the comfort of her presence.

His forehead wrinkled in thought. "Listen, girl, you gotta do something about that Cass."

"Cass?" Gayle blinked over the sudden change of topic.

"He's always jumped into any idiotic thing that came into his mind—no nerves, that boy. I always thought that mountain climbing of his was a pretty risky, useless way to waste time."

"I agree that it's dangerous, but I suppose Search and Rescue is a community service, not useless."

"Humph! Most people call collecting for the March of Dimes a community service. Cass, he *likes* risking his fool neck."

Gayle lifted her shoulders. "He's a big boy now, I don't know how anyone can stop him from doing what he likes."

"Can't you understand plain English, girl? I don't want anyone to stop him! I want someone to get him back up there again!" His skin had turned dusky from emotion, and he gasped for oxygen again. "If Cass doesn't climb another mountain pretty soon, he'll end up living with fear the rest of his life. And that'd be a cryin' shame."

Gayle thought for a moment, then shook her head. "No, I can't believe that. We were at Blodgett Canyon, and he didn't so much as act nervous when he told me about his accident."

"Well, naturally he'd hide his fear around you, girl. It ain't manly."

"For heaven's sake, ideas like that went out with the Dark Ages."

"Not in the country, they didn't."

"Even if he is afraid, I don't know why you think I can do anything about it." Gayle stood up, preparing to leave.

Harvey gave her a sly look. "Cass, he's always come to visit me regular, but lately our conversations have been mostly about my purty redheaded nurse. So I figure you're the best bet for talkin' him out of his spooks."

She stopped at the door and gave a laugh of disbelief. "Surely, you don't actually expect *me*—of all people—to talk Cass into climbing back up a mountain?"

Gayle had a couple of free hours before seeing her next patient, so she decided to drop in at Hudson's Hair, as instructed by Hilda. A bell jangled when she opened the door. Lush vines hung in macramé hangers against tasteful wallpaper. The chairs in all three stations were occupied. A couple of women were seated at the hair dryers too. The babble of feminine chatter stopped when Gayle walked in.

"Hi, I'm Carla Hudson." The woman behind the desk had a friendly smile. "And you must be Gayle Stromm. I've been wanting to get a look at you."

"So much for incognito," Gayle said with an answering smile. "When can I get a haircut?"

"I can do you now." Carla evicted the young woman idling in a chair, and fastened a cape around Gayle's neck, running expert fingers through her hair. "You've got the wrong haircut for natural curl. Do you trust me?"

At Gayle's tentative nod, she tilted the chair back and began the shampoo. "I've been wanting to meet you, because small-town people don't think much of us big-city aliens. We have to stick together."

One of the women lounging by the hair dryers

walked over to lean against the pebbled-glass divider between the chairs. "I heard that," she said with a laugh.

"This is Bonnie Breckenridge," Carla said, bringing the chair upright and vigorously toweling Gayle's hair. "She's with Ritz Realty."

Oh, no, Gayle thought. That Breckenridge girl. The main contender for Cass, and the last person in town she wanted to meet. "Hi, Bonnie," she said cautiously.

"Hi, Gayle." Bonnie was in her late twenties, with a petite body, chestnut hair, a wholesome face, and an appealing grin. "I think we country mice have been very tolerant toward you city mice, where our men are concerned."

Gayle squinted through the wet hair hanging in front of her eyes, silently cursing Hilda for getting her into this. "You're in real estate, are you? I'll be putting my house up for sale pretty soon."

"I'd love to sell your house. I'd fatten my purse, and as a bonus I'd be hurrying you out of town and weeding out the competition." Bonnie gave a good-natured laugh.

Gayle couldn't help laughing too. "Believe me, you country mice don't have anything to worry about."

Carla finished the cut and did magic with a hand-held dryer, then handed Gayle a mirror. "What do you think?"

She stared at herself, turning this way and that. Her hair was still shoulder length but was feathered around the face, the rest tousled in a disciplined way. When she shook her head, every curl fell naturally back in place. "It's great!"

Bonnie studied her. "Too great. I'd better keep an eye on you. How would you like to come down to the Brass Rail tonight? We're having girls' night out. Just turn up there at about eight."

The other young women in the shop had been following the conversation. "Yes, please come," they broke in.

Gayle hesitated for only a moment, then smiled. "Sure, why not? I'd love to."

Gayle turned up at the Brass Rail at about eight. Before going inside, she glanced at her dark blue leggings and oversize flowered sweater and wondered if she looked too much like a city mouse. Deciding it was useless to worry over it, she entered the folksy saloon, which was already crowded and noisy with the clanging of a group of one-armed poker machines. The "girls" were gathered around a table, sharing a pizza and a pitcher of beer.

They were so enthusiastically friendly that Gayle's sense of strangeness vanished immediately. Her stressed, overwound internal spring began to relax. In no time she was digging into the pizza and beer and either groaning or dissolving in laughter over tales of work, bosses, families, and the foibles of past or present boyfriends.

By nine the place was noisy to the point of rowdiness, with a combo playing country-western music in competition with the clamor of the poker machines. The small dance floor was packed with couples. No one at Gayle's table was dancing, since a group of women seemed to be too formidable for the men to approach. But they were having a wonderful time on their own. Then Carla glanced toward the door and grinned. "Here comes trouble."

Everyone fell silent and turned their heads in unison. Gayle's heart jumped. Cass was threading his way across the crowded room, looking devastating in a tan western jacket and a white shirt, open at the neck. She quickly turned away, praying he wouldn't be so tactless as to come to a table where both she and Bonnie were sitting.

But apparently the situation didn't bother him in the slightest. "Hey, this is my kind of party," he said with a big grin, and twirled a chair around from another table, nudging himself in among the women. He straddled the chair, and the silence dissolved into a babble of laughter and bantering. He didn't single out any one woman, but Gayle could feel his gaze light on her too often for comfort, even though she kept her attention riveted to her mug.

When the band began playing another number, Cass swung Carla out on the floor. Gayle propped her elbow on the table and shielded her eyes, surreptitiously watching them. She felt absurdly jealous to see his tall, muscular body move against another woman; she didn't think she could have stood it if he'd asked Bonnie to dance first.

Once Cass had crashed the all-woman table, a couple of other men claimed dancing partners. Gayle moved into an empty chair next to Bonnie and said, "You knew Cass was coming when you asked me along tonight, didn't you?"

"Sure, everyone turns up here sooner or later. Don't let either him or me spoil your fun. Think of it this way, it's always a good idea to analyze the competition."

Gayle wasn't sure if she was teasing or serious. "Look, I'm not interested in Cass. You don't have to worry about me."

"Honey, I've been running after Cass so long, it's become a hopeless habit, so I know when to worry. I've never known him to act like a poleaxed steer before, which is what he's been doing ever since you came to town." Bonnie took a sip of beer, then laughed. "And of course you're interested in him, silly. Everyone's interested in Cass."

Apparently Bonnie didn't have a vindictive bone in her body, so Gayle laughed with relief. "Actually, I doubt that he's very affected by either one of us. Seeing as we're both sitting here like wallflowers."

"Why, you're absolutely right, we are, aren't we? Men! Who can understand the critters?"

Just then Jackson, Cass's partner, came up to the table. Struggling with the agony of shyness, he motioned for Bonnie to dance. They'd only just whirled onto the floor when Gayle looked up in surprise at a touch on her shoulder.

"Hi," Cass said, smiling down at her. "Care to take a spin around the floor?"

"I thought you were dancing with Carla."

"Someone else took over—so how about it?"

"Why not?"

Her heart leaped in anticipation as she put her hands in his, allowing him to pull her to her feet. He led her through the crush to the small floor and put his arm around her waist, pulling her close. She put her arm around his neck, the corduroy of his jacket velvety against her skin. He moved with fluid grace against her. The sensation of being dainty and fragile, her hand tiny in his huge paw, drove everything else out of her mind—the people, the music, the jangle of the poker machines.

"You look awfully nice," he said, after forging a space on the crowded floor by whirling her around. "Is there something different about your hair?"

"I had it cut and styled by an expert," Gayle said, enormously pleased that he'd noticed. "Do you like it?"

"Mmm-m, let's have a look." He examined her face closely with a warm, sultry gaze. "Makes those gray eyes of yours look as big as perky saucers. Yup, I like it."

"Thank goodness, I was afraid I wouldn't pass muster."

"Oh, my yes, do you ever." Cass pulled her closer. Her bones felt as if they were turning to liquid, and she was amazed her legs could hold her upright, much less move in rhythm with the music.

"It was a bit of a surprise to see you and Bonnie sitting at the same table," he murmured against her ear.

"Oh, was it now? Why?"

"Maybe I was curious about what you were talking about before Jackson broke up your conversation. I may have been wondering if you were comparing notes."

"What makes you think we were talking about you?" She lifted a brow. "Is your ego working overtime again?"

He made a face. "What were you talking about, then?"

"About the price of rice in China," she said, and laughed softly. "And . . . you."

"Mmm-hmmm!" Delight gleamed in his eyes.

After only a few moments the number ended. Cass moved her to the sidelines and held her close with an arm around her waist.

"Do you know anything about Jackson asking Bonnie to dance?" Gayle asked, bending a suspicious eye at him. "He didn't act as if it was his idea."

"It wasn't. I bribed him to, so I wouldn't get in trouble by asking you."

"Honestly, Cass, you're incorrigible! I suppose you bribed someone to cut in on you and Carla too."

"She was smart enough to figure things out herself and told me to go for it," he said blithely. "And it wasn't so much bribing Jackson as spurring him on. He's been smitten with Bonnie for years, but is too shy to do anything about it."

"Bonnie is smitten with you, and Jackson is smitten with her? I can't believe this!" Gayle said, shaking her head. "Life in a small town is like a soap opera."

"You've got it."

When the band began playing again, he pulled her close with both arms around her waist. She wrapped her arms around his neck, very aware of the satiny feel of his smooth-shaven cheek against hers as they danced. "Are you having fun?" His whispered question tickled her ear and sent vibrations rushing through her body.

"Yes," she murmured against his neck, feeling lighter and happier than she had in years, in all her life. "Oh, yes."

"So am I." He was moving his feet in tiny steps, caressing the full length of his body against hers. "This is quite a novelty for me, you know."

Pulling away, she looked questioningly at him. "What do you mean?"

He grinned down at her. "I'm such a big dude that this is the first time I've ever danced cheek to cheek with a woman."

She laughed and pressed her cheek against his again. "I don't think you're too big, you're just perfect. Most of the time when I dance, I have to look down at a man's head. It's embarrassing when I see that he's got dandruff, or a bald spot starting."

Cass gave a whoop of laughter. "Well, thank goodness you're down there and I'm up here."

They didn't talk after that, just moved slowly, at one with each other, alone in the crowd. When the number ended, Cass held her close when she tried to pull away. "I'd like to go on dancing with you like this all night," he said softly. "But I have to warn you, people are bound to talk if I don't take you back to the table and spread my attention around. It'll be a statement if we go on dancing. Would that bother you?"

She stared up at him, struggling with the demanding needs he'd awakened in her body during the dance. If she danced with him the rest of the night, she could guess where they would most certainly end up later. If that happened, she wouldn't be a challenge any longer, and he'd lose interest. Then she'd end up like Bonnie, watching him flit from woman to woman.

"I'd better go back to the table," she said in a husky, reluctant voice. "And you'd better dance with Bonnie to even things out."

For an instant she thought she saw hurt, maybe even anger, flash in his eyes. "Okay, if that's the way you want it," he said in a controlled voice, and maneuvered her through the couples and back to the table.

Gayle decided she must have been mistaken about the emotion in his eyes, because he was grinning when he pulled Bonnie out of her chair. He was laughing when he whirled her around and swept his corner of the dance floor clear in an exuberant polka.

After a few moments Gayle couldn't watch any longer. She slipped out of the Brass Rail without anyone noticing and went home.

Six

Though the next day was Saturday, Gayle got out of bed before nine. She couldn't sleep. She'd awakened all too often during the night, tormented by erotic desires she didn't want to feel. The only good part of it was that her preoccupation with the scent and feel of Cass hadn't left room for nightmares.

"How much do you want to bet," she said to her bleary face in the mirror, "that that infuriating man is going to sleep like a baby until noon?"

Trudging out to the kitchen, she breakfasted on a toasted English muffin and coffee. She should have been making plans to refinish the gouged, grimy wood cabinets, but it was too bright and sunny outside the open window over the sink to think of work. A balmy May breeze wafted in to stir her hair. It was a perfect day for . . . a picnic.

Giving a cry of impatience, she grabbed the phone and dialed Portland, hoping the sound of her mother's voice would bring back her sanity. "Hi, Mom."

"Gayle, darling! How are you?"

Inexplicably, tears came to her eyes, and she said quickly, "I'm fine."

Mother's intuition sprang into action. "Something's wrong, isn't it? You sound funny."

Equally as inexplicably, she couldn't bring herself to tell her mother about her troublesome attraction to Cass. "I'm okay, honest. I've made friends with some other women, and the end of the remodeling is in sight."

They talked about the house for a while, then her mother said, "I wish I could come and help you finish up."

"I wish you could come, because I miss you." Gayle's eyes teared up again. "I need to get out of here and come home to Portland."

"Something *is* wrong. If I know you, you're working too hard. Honestly, Gayle, I told you it wasn't necessary to drop everything and fix up that house for me!" The sound of an exaggerated sigh came over the lines. "I just don't understand where you got this idea that you have to single-handedly save the world."

Gayle made a face and derailed the old, familiar lecture by asking for all the gossip from home.

After she hung up, she realized her mood had lightened. She donned a pair of white shorts and a flowered, sleeveless blouse, put on a little makeup, and ran a wire brush through her new hairdo. She decided to do something less demanding than the kitchen cabinets—preferably something outside in the spring air. Pacing around the yard with a third cup of coffee in her hand, she walked to the brink of her back hillside. Her gaze zeroed in on Cass's house across the valley.

"Stop that!" she whispered, and looked instead at the tiny stream at the base of her yard and the field beyond that. The view was almost laughably pastoral, with two Herefords and several horses grazing on the haze of new green under last year's dry brown grass.

Killdeers were making a strident fuss, trying to protect their ground nests.

Gayle's eye lit on the heap of dead knapweeds piled in the far corner of her yard, and she remembered Harvey's advice. That was it—a good bonfire would take her mind off Cass.

She didn't have kerosene, but paint thinner was just as combustible. She brought that and a book of matches down the hill to the pile of weeds. Just to be on the safe side, she unearthed an old hose in the garage and hooked it to the outside faucet. After liberally sprinkling paint thinner, she tossed on several lighted matches and watched with a sense of satisfaction as the tinder-dry knapweeds flared up.

Her satisfaction turned into twinges of anxiety when the breeze whipped up the flames, yanking the billowing white smoke this way and that. Running back to the house, she turned on the faucet. To her dismay water sprayed out of the ruptured sides of the hose, with only a weak arc spouting out the end. There wasn't nearly enough force to reach what was rapidly becoming a crackling conflagration.

Anxiety turned into frank worry when the fire began eating into the dead grass beyond her yard. She breathed a sigh of relief when it stopped at the stream.

Then, to her horror, the breeze playfully grabbed an explosion of sparks, flinging them over the creek into the dry grass of the pasture. Flames burst up in several spots, creating a smudge of black smoke.

"Oh, my God!" Gayle cried out when the spots joined into a solid line of orange flames, rapidly advancing toward the cows and horses.

Bounding up the hill to the house, she raced into the kitchen and called the fire department. Then she raced back out of the house and stood on the hill, wringing her hands. Within seconds the central fire siren began hooting. Sirens wailed from every direction around the city, as the volunteer fire fighters began their run.

But they were a long way off yet. And the fire was already halfway across the field. The horses had galloped out of danger, but the two confused Herefords were pressed against the fence in front of the advancing blaze. She didn't think the firemen would come in time to save them.

Running down the hill, Gayle leaped the stream and climbed through the barbed-wire fence. She raced along the perimeter of the blackened area. The fire was roaring at her heels when she reached the Herefords. Black smoke billowed around her, stinging her eyes and burning her throat. "Shoo! Scat! Move!" she shouted frantically, trying to chase the cows to the leeward side of the field. But they only pressed themselves tighter against the fence.

"What in the devil are you doing?!"

The sound of the human shout jerked her around. She went weak with relief to see help arriving. Though it seemed an odd coincidence that help was in the form of Cass, with a funny-looking hard hat on his head and a shovel in his hand. His yellow coat was flying out behind him as he pelted across the field, forging through the smoke in ten-foot strides.

"Hurry!" she screamed. "I can't make these cows move!"

"Forget those damn cows and get the hell out of here!" he bellowed. A resounding clunk of his shovel on each Hereford rump sent them hightailing toward the horses.

Grabbing Gayle's arm, he dragged her at a gallop out of the path of the fire. "That was the most moronic thing I've ever seen anyone try!" he raged, goose-stepping her up the field toward her house.

"Will you stop ranting at me!" she shouted, jerking

her arm away from his hand. "I'm not so moronic as you seem to think! I was watching the fire! I could have gotten out of the way."

"You're so moronic, you didn't even realize the danger you were in!"

She glared at him, wondering why he had showed up so inopportunely, just in time to witness her stupidity. "What are you doing here anyway?"

"What am I doing here? You called me, for the love of mud! I'm a fireman. Why do you think I'm wearing this stupid outfit?"

"Oh."

When Gayle was out of range of the fire, Cass ran back with his shovel and disappeared into the thick black smoke. Only then did she began to understand the worry and fear that must have initiated his rage.

She felt an enormous sense of relief when a swarm of volunteer firemen arrived to fan out around the edge of the flaming circle. Seconds later a fire engine bounced down her hill. Another one came in from the other side of the field, and the men began hosing water on the fire, turning the boiling black smoke white. After that, the grass fire was quickly put out. And within an hour everyone had left.

Everyone except Cass. Folding his arms over his chest, he glowered at Gayle from under his hard hat. His face, hands, jeans, and yellow coat were smudged with soot.

Humiliated over the situation she had caused, Gayle hid her face with her hands for a moment, then pulled them away far enough to look up at him over the tops of her fingers. "Just don't start hollering at me again," she said defensively.

"You deserve to be hollered at! What possessed you to start a grass fire?"

"I did not deliberately set out to cause a grass fire!" she exclaimed. "Harvey Fenster told me everyone

STORMY'S MAN • 79

burns their knapweeds, so I . . ." She let that line of
reasoning drop, wishing she hadn't brought it up.

"Harvey!" Cass lifted one of his lowered brows. "You
ran right out and started a fire because Harvey told
you to?"

She made a face and shrugged slightly. "What can
I say?"

Pulling up one corner of his mouth, he snorted a
laugh. "Every spring we have around here what's
known as the Great Bitterroot Valley Burn. Harvey's
right—everyone does burn their knapweeds . . .
and their sheds, their fences, and sometimes their
houses along with them. Last time he lit a match to
his, he burned up his haystack. I don't suppose he
told you that?"

"No, he didn't," Gayle said sheepishly.

Cass's face turned red with anger again. "Do you
have any idea how I felt when I saw you prancing
around down there with flames licking at your butt?"

"Will you kindly just drop the subject of me and
that fire!" she snarled between gritted teeth. "I'm
mortified enough without you rubbing salt in the
wound. What's the matter with you anyway?"

"What's the matter with me? Me!" Suddenly, his
face collapsed, the anger draining out. "Oh, God!
When I saw you in front of that fire . . . I didn't
think I could get there fast enough, and—"

Lunging forward, Cass hauled her into his arms.
His hard hat fell off when he pressed his face into her
neck. "I have never *ever* been so scared in my entire
life!" he whispered against the quickening pulse
above her collarbone. "You could have been *killed*!"

Astonished, Gayle stood crushed against his body,
barely able to breathe, her arms trapped against her
sides by his fierce embrace. Her lips were pressed
against his tousled hair, and her nose was quivering

at his tantalizing mixture of scents: sweat, smoke, masculinity, and his lemony shaving lotion.

As quickly as he'd grabbed her, Cass let her go again, and backed off to rub his face with both hands, smearing the black. "Sorry about that," he said, as though equally surprised by the intensity of his reaction. "I got you all dirty."

Gayle looked down at the smudges of black on her white shorts and flowered blouse. "It doesn't matter. I don't care."

He let his gaze run back down over her skimpy outfit. A teasing sparkle regenerated in his eyes, and his drawl came back when he said, "It sure would have been a shame if you'd bar-bee-cued those spectacular legs, Stormy. Shorts must have been invented for tall women like you."

"Don't be silly." With a mixture of pleasure and embarrassment Gayle sat down on one of the huge boulders by the side of the house. She braced her feet on the side, and wrapped her arms around her knees.

Cass tossed off his coat and sat on the boulder next to her, his shoulder almost but not quite brushing hers. "Why did you sneak away from the Brass Rail last night?"

The change of topic took her off guard. "You already had a harem to keep you busy, Cass," she said, giving a short laugh. "I didn't see any point in me sticking around and probably end up falling in love with you along with all the rest," she added without thinking.

His chin jerked up, and a playful breeze fanned his hair over his forehead. He studied her face intently for a moment. "Are you saying you're falling in love with me too?"

Wincing, she cursed herself for trying to be flip with a touchy subject, and backpedaled as fast as she could. "Well . . . on the edge . . . maybe. For heaven's sake, Cass, I was just making a joke." Frowning, she replayed what he'd just said. "What do you mean—'too'?"

"I mean, me too."

Staring at him sidelong, she couldn't quite absorb what he was saying. "You, too . . . what?"

Pushing his hands into his jeans pockets, he hunched his shoulders and smiled. "It seems as if I'm on the edge of falling in love with you, too, Stormy."

Gayle looked for duplicity in his face, but his expression was simply quizzical, and his brown eyes were warm enough to melt her. In the lengthening silence the singing of two bluebirds by their fence-post house seemed too sweet to bear. "On the edge . . . ?" she repeated softly.

He nodded solemnly. "Right on the brink of the point of no return."

"With me?" she asked, wondering why a man like Cass would be drawn to a flamingo when he could have any swan he wanted. "Why me?"

Glancing first at her long legs, then caressing her face with his gaze, he laughed softly. "I don't know. Probably because you're the only woman I know who'd risk her life for a couple of brainless cows. How about you? Why me?"

Gayle took a turn at looking over his rugged, black-smudged face; his broad-shouldered body in his plaid shirt, suspenders, and jeans. Her inner feelings, the desire he made her feel, all of it was too new to comprehend, much less explain. "Lord only knows," she murmured, shaking her head.

His laugh was so appealing, she actually felt faint. "Maybe it's your honesty I love," he said. "This is really fascinating, isn't it, Stormy?"

"I guess, sort of, Starbaugh." So fascinating, her heart was full to overflowing with it. "Too bad nothing can ever come of it," she said, as much to herself as him.

He lifted his head and looked up into the blue sky, frowning as he watched a hawk soaring in a circle. Then he looked at Gayle. "Are you certain nothing can come of us?"

Very reluctantly, she said, "Have you ever known two people so mismatched as you and I?"

He frowned for a few moments longer, then nodded. "I suppose you're right, but it might be fun to explore the possibilities."

"That's the problem, Cass, you're into fun and games. And I'm a serious person, scared of getting hurt."

He studied the curves and features of her face. "I think you must have been in love before and got hurt—is that why you're afraid of this?"

"No, I've never been in love before. I just know how it'd be."

"That's interesting," he said. "I've never been in love before either."

Surprised, she searched his face. "From what I've heard, I thought you would have been in and out of love like a yo-yo."

"Nah, not hardly." Shifting restlessly on the boulder, he stretched his legs out and crossed them. "I've always run scared from anything that might tie me down."

"Why?"

He stared at the blackened circle in the brown field below the hill and shrugged, acting as leery as she had of revealing too much. "Maybe I'm scared of being hurt too." He quickly retreated from that admission, grinning. "Or maybe because there's a whole world waiting to be explored, and a thousand things I haven't experienced yet."

"And mountains to be climbed?" she murmured, reminding herself of their differences.

He glanced at and quickly away from the Bitterroots towering above the valley. "And mountains to be climbed."

Cass's guarded expression led her to wonder if Harvey was right about his fear of the cliff. She began to suspect he was hiding a complex, mysterious man under his frivolous exterior. All the more reason for her to be cautious, she told herself. "Falling in love is a serious business, with a whole new set of circumstances to consider. At least that's how I see it. Are you into permanent relationships?"

He pursed his lips, looking uncomfortable.

"That's what I thought," she said, beginning to feel a little desperate. "I suppose some people can take these things lightly, but I'm not that type."

Cass bent down to pick up a small stone, examined it, and tossed it down the hill. "So, what do you suggest we do about this little problem of ours?"

She smiled. "Well, it isn't really a problem yet, thank goodness. But if it should turn into one, I expect it'll solve itself when I sell the house and go back to Portland."

"I suppose." He watched with interest as she unfolded her long legs and stretched them out beside his. "But you'll be here for several weeks before you can get this house sold, Stormy. What do we do until then?"

She stared at his enormous work boots, which made her running shoes look tiny. "We'll just have to stay away from each other, I guess."

"But I've been trying to do that ever since I first saw you," he said, snorting a laugh. "And it hasn't worked worth a damn. All I think about is you."

"You do?" she murmured, gazing at his grimy face.

"Yep, and we always seem to be running into each

other," he said, a smile twitching at his lips. "Like last night at the Brass Rail. I couldn't sleep because I kept seeing you in my mind, remembering the feel of you in my àrms when we danced. That's how I happened to be out and about so early on a Saturday morning, and consequently got here first when you staged your fire."

"You were awake last night too?"

He nodded slowly, and her entire body came alive under his heavy-lidded, very warm scrutiny.

Slapping the boulder they were sitting on, Gayle exclaimed impatiently, "None of this would've happened if you hadn't dumped these rocks in my yard and blackmailed me into going on the picnic with you. That's why we're in trouble—you couldn't leave well enough alone."

"I'll admit my guilt in doing that. Unfortunately, I'm not as good at solutions as I am at initiating problems," he said, touching a fingertip to her knee. "Do you have any suggestions?"

The sensation of his grazing touch spread instantly up her thigh and into the soft areas of her body. She flicked his hand away. "I generally solve all my problems by working until I'm too exhausted to think about them."

"You've been doing that already, it seems to me," he drawled. "Has it worked?"

She shook her head. "Not very well."

Cass clasped his fingers around a knee and rocked back on the boulder, never taking his gaze off her. "Since it isn't working for us to stay away from each other, maybe we should try a three-hundred-sixty-degree turnabout, and glut ourselves."

"What do you mean?"

He grinned. "See each other every chance we can."

She looked at him skeptically. "I've been talking about nipping this thing in the bud. If we do what you're suggesting, we'll end up fertilizing it into full bloom."

He laughed. "You have the most suspicious mind I've ever run across. I'm only suggesting that we talk and get to know each other. Backgrounds, that sort of thing. They say familiarity breeds contempt."

Gayle laughed. "Who's this 'they,' and how'd they figure that out?"

"I don't know, exactly," Cass admitted cheerfully. "How about it, Stormy? I'd like to take you out to dinner tonight. Are you game to give it a try?"

"Well . . . I don't know." Every fiber in Gayle's being warned her against it. But she simply couldn't shape her mouth to say no, even though she suspected he was playing games with her. "Oh, all right, I'll go out to dinner with you—just this once." She touched her finger to the muscular arm supporting his bent leg. "But I'd better see some contempt developing, or everything is off."

Seven

At five that afternoon Gayle immersed her too-tall body in the too-short tub of her newly redecorated bathroom, and contemplated her fate.

A dozen times during the day she'd picked up the phone but hadn't been able to bring herself to make the cancellation call. A hundred times she'd wondered what had possessed her to give in to Cass's ridiculous scheme.

It was easy to swallow every word that came off his seductive lips, while looking into those sultry eyes. But did she truly believe he was falling in love with her? She gave a wistful laugh. No, he was simply heating up his campaign. Which mountain climber was it—Hillary?—who answered, "Because it's there," when asked why he wanted to climb Everest? Cass would say anything short of proposing marriage to conquer Gayle.

She stared at her knees, steepled out of a froth of fragrant bubbles. Considering the reaction of her restless nerve endings to the touch of silky water, she suspected his conquest would be fulfilled tonight.

She had two no-win choices, as far as she could

see. She could hold herself back and end up with heartbreak and regrets. Or she could give herself and reap heartbreak and some sweet, spectacular memories. "Damned if you do, and damned if you don't," she murmured, but in her heart she'd already made the choice.

After toweling herself dry, Gayle made up her face. She scowled at her freckles and cursed Mendel's law for cheating her out of the beauty genes in her family. The best she could do was play up her large gray eyes. Then she fastened her hair up on her head in a mass of coppery curls and feathered some strands around her face.

After spraying herself with a flowery perfume, she agonized over what to wear. Finally, she decided to put on an outfit her sister had given her. Margo had worlds more experience and fashion sense, she told herself, slipping into the beautifully draped shell-pink silk blouse and skirt.

After putting on some gold jewelry and shoes with just a tiny heel, she decided everything was all wrong. She was ready to change when she heard Cass's rat-a-tat on the front door. "Oh, no!" she said with a groan, wishing she'd followed through with the cancellation call.

Heart thudding, she trudged down the hall like a doomed prisoner walking that last mile, and opened the door.

"Hello there, Stormy," he said, a grin on his face. His fingers were tucked in the pockets of sharply creased tan slacks, and his brown tweed sport jacket was tailored to fit his broad shoulders perfectly. He even had on a paisley tie with his pale yellow dress shirt, and his sun-streaked hair was newly cut. It touched her to see he'd taken some extra pains with his appearance too.

The cockiness faded out of his grin as his gaze

moved from the blazing hair piled on her head, down over her body, and back up to her face. He pulled his hands out of his pockets and buttoned one button of his jacket. "You're so beautiful, it almost hurts to look at you."

His extravagant compliment whisked all her reservations away. Warmth and happiness curled through her. "You look pretty handsome yourself," she said, a smile trembling on her lips.

"It'd take a lot of handsome to balance out such a vision as you."

They smiled inanely at each other for a few moments, then Cass said, "Well . . . mmm-hmmm . . . are you ready and raring to go then?"

"Oh, I'm raring all right." She ran to the bedroom for a clutch purse and jacket, then ran back, her heart thumping over what was to come. "Now I'm ready too."

Cass scowled as they walked toward the pickup. "You look too nice to ride in this rig. I should have gone out and bought a car today."

The truck was waxed and polished, its chrome gleaming in the setting sun. "No, I like it." Stretching her legs out in the ample space, she flashed him a teasing glance. "I feel like Cinderella in a pumpkin."

Cass ran around and got in. "What does that make me—the rat turned into a coachman?" He looked at her, his arms braced against the wheel. "Or Prince Charming?"

She laughed. "Just as long as you aren't the fairy godmother."

He groaned. "Oh, you're quick on the uptake tonight, aren't you, Stormy? Now I suppose I'll have to take you right back into the house and prove myself."

"No, no, I'll take your word for it."

"Nuts!" he said, snapping his fingers. "But if this is

any example of how the evening is going to go, then you'd better watch out, lady."

"If I'm going to stay a lady, I guess I'd better."

Cass laughed and started the pickup. When he headed down the highway, Gayle asked, "Where are you taking me?"

"I know a nice place down Sula way. That's a small town near the pass into Idaho. About an hour away."

"An *hour* away? How far is an hour?"

"No one counts miles in Big Sky Country. Everything is so far, it's intimidating." He glanced anxiously at her. "Is an hour farther than you want to go with me?"

"No, that's fine." Gayle felt so happy at that moment, she would have gladly traveled to the ends of the earth with him.

"I hope you like the place," he said, still frowning anxiously.

"Why wouldn't I?"

"I don't know." After a few minutes of silence Cass launched into a running monologue about the history of the small towns they were passing. When the valley became narrower and wilder, with the mountains closing in, he told about Indian battles, and trappers coming to fur rendezvous.

Smiling, Gayle watched his face as he talked, only half listening. Everything about him seemed so appealing: the strength of his profile, the laughter and fun in his eyes, his smile, his interest in anything and everything.

Suddenly, he stopped in midsentence. "I'm boring you."

"No, you aren't. I love hearing you talk."

"If you love it so much, what's the last thing I said?"

She opened her mouth but couldn't scratch up a hint of what it might have been.

He nodded. "I knew it! I'm boring you. When I get nervous, I talk too much."

"You're nervous?" Gayle exclaimed, astonished. "You?"

"Me." He flexed his fingers on the wheel and gave a laugh. "Every time I'm around you, I feel as if something momentous ought to take place, and I'm afraid I'll blow it. If I don't shut up, I will for a fact. You haven't had a chance to say a word since we hit the road."

She laughed, too, perplexed by this unexpected facet of Cass. "When I get nervous, I can't think of anything to say, so I'm delighted to be with someone who is willing to fill the silences. And you aren't boring, it's just that I was more interested in watching you talk than in what you were saying."

His eyes sparkled as he glanced at her. "Now there's a mixed compliment if ever I've heard one."

"Think of it this way, you can tell me that stuff all over again another time, and I won't know the difference."

"Hmmm," he commented. "You won't have to worry about that this time, though, because here we are."

Gayle climbed down out of the pickup and looked around. The lodge was set in a narrow canyon, surrounded by stately pines. The mountain behind it was silhouetted against the tail end of a ruddy sunset. The river ran singing past.

Cass escorted her into a restaurant with a cozily formal atmosphere: linen tablecloths, candles, real flowers, and gleaming crystal. The owner greeted Cass warmly, and seated them at a prime table in a private corner, beside an enormous window with a full view of the mountain and river.

"I never know what to expect from you," she said after ordering, grateful she'd had sense enough to put on so dressy a dress. "I wasn't prepared for anything so elegant."

"That's my aim, to keep you off balance and curious."

"You're doing a good job of it."

"Yea-ah," he said, grinning, and lifted his glass of wine. "Here's to us. And to contempt."

She laughed and raised her glass. "To contempt."

His eyes sparkled. "Or whatever else might happen between us."

Breathlessly, she touched her glass to his and sipped. Excited by the possibilities of what he'd just said, Gayle became even more acutely aware of the broad shoulders under his tweed jacket, his deep chest, and the pulse in his throat.

After they'd made the rounds at the salad bar, she held her fork motionless, watching Cass eat. The appetite of so big and energetic a man was awesome, even provocative, to her. When she began wondering if he fed his other hungers as vigorously, her face flushed hot. She quickly took a bite of lettuce and asked a question off the top of her head: "Where did you go to college, Cass?"

He glanced up, surprised. "What makes you think this country boy went to college?"

"Oh, I don't know. Your Montana drawl comes and goes. Sometimes when you don't remember to use it, I thought I detected a little educational smoothing."

He popped an olive into his mouth and grinned. "You caught me. By some fluke I earned a full scholarship in high school, and it would have been a waste not to use it. So I took a degree in geology from the School of Mines at Golden, Colorado. But after I graduated, I quickly figured out I'd go crazy pushing papers around a desk for the rest of my life. I can't stand being cooped up. I stuck with it long enough to save up enough money to buy into Jackson's daddy's excavating business. He was sort of a father to me, too, so he gave me a good deal."

She studied his face. "You have more 'sort of' relatives than anyone I ever met. What about your real family?"

"Sort-of relatives are all I have," he answered, and turned his head away to look out the window. The sunset had faded to black, and enormous stars were shining in the sky over the mountain.

When he didn't elaborate, she said, "I'm sorry, I shouldn't have asked. It's none of my business."

He brought his attention back to her. "Maybe it is, and maybe it isn't."

Gayle had no idea what he meant by that, and breathed a sigh of relief when the waitress arrived to serve their meals and extricate her from an uncomfortable silence.

Cass cut into his prime rib and ate hungrily for a few minutes, his forehead creased thoughtfully. Then he laid down his fork and leaned his elbows on the table, hands clasped under his chin. "My father was a handyman, of sorts. He couldn't bear to stay in one place more than a year, or two at the longest."

Gayle had been lifting a bite of roasted lamb toward her mouth. Her fork froze in place as she stared at him. She hadn't expected him to answer. "That sounds like a tough life for a child."

He nodded slowly. "Even tougher for a woman. My mother got sick of moving around and ran off with another man when I was seven. Then it was only my dad and me. We came to Hamilton a year later, and he was killed in a construction accident."

Suddenly, it became clear to her; no wonder he was so leery about commitment, when he'd lost everyone he'd loved as a child. She put down her fork and reached out to circle her fingers around his wrist. "Oh, Cass, that's so sad."

He took her hand between his for a moment, then gave it back to her, declining the sympathy he saw in her face. "It wasn't that sad, so eat your dinner before it gets cold." He ate a few bites of everything on his plate, then looked up. "It wasn't sad, it was probably the best thing that ever happened to me. The authorities couldn't locate my mother, or any natural family, so Jackson's parents took me in."

"They adopted you?"

"Can you imagine anyone in their right mind adopting me?" he said, laughing. Then he turned serious again. "They couldn't, because my family wasn't around to sign me over. It was a foster-home situation instead, but they didn't need an official document telling them to care. Actually, the whole town ended up making me their own. Country people have a lot of sympathy for stray dogs and orphans."

Gayle wondered if that flip observation revealed more than Cass cared to admit about his feelings. Since he'd made it clear he didn't want pity, she picked up her fork and put a piece of lamb into her mouth, rather than reaching out to him. "Yes, I've seen how warm people are, even in the short time I've been here."

"Uh-huh, I felt welcome in any home I walked into. When I turned into a hell-raising adolescent and frazzled everyone's nerves, I had more parents, grandparents, uncles, and aunts coming down on me than you can imagine." He put his last forkful of mashed potatoes and gravy into his mouth. "I must have lived in three dozen homes during my teen years. I was growing so fast and was always so hungry, I figured no one could afford to feed me for longer than a month or two at a time. Consequently, I have the largest extended family known to mankind."

"Sort of," she murmured, smiling.

"Sort of," Cass picked up a twisted orange slice, all that was left on his plate, and nipped the meat away from the rind with even white teeth. "Now, I've revealed all, so it's your turn. Tell me your life history."

Though he had finished with his meal, Gayle had only begun hers. She concentrated on buttering her baked potato, not half as eager to talk about her life history as to listen to his. "I was born in Portland and never lived anywhere else. My father was a supervisor at a lumber company, and my mother stayed at home. Consequently, she had a hard time when my dad fell in love with another woman and divorced her. She didn't have any job training to fall back on."

"I'll bet that was rough," he said, gazing at her with understanding. "I think I remember you talking about a sister once."

"I have two. They're both married and juggling glamour careers. One's a model, and the other acts in TV commercials. Being a nurse doesn't sound like much compared to their careers, but it was what I always wanted, so that's what I did."

"Lucky for me you did," he murmured, smiling. "I wouldn't have had much use for a model or a TV actress after my accident."

Gayle laughed. "Lucky—what rubbish! You were hollering your head off about me throwing you around like a hurricane."

"I mean I'm lucky to know you, now that I'm strong enough to protect myself," he said, grinning. "Do your sisters look like you?"

Now they were getting into a gray area she didn't care to share with a man like Cass. She lifted her wineglass and sipped, then put it down precisely at the top of her plate. "My mother is small and petite, with nice, smooth dark hair and a perfectly beautiful face. She's still lovely at forty-six. My sisters look just like her. My father is a big, tall redheaded German. Unfortunately, I took after him."

"Personally, I think you're the lucky one," Cass said.

"Personally, I think you're probably the only one in the world who does." She hoped she was doing as well as he had about hiding painful feelings. Playing tough guy, she took a bite of her potato and tossed out her old standby: "I'm just a flamingo hatched out in a nest of swans."

When Cass didn't comment, she glanced up. "You're supposed to laugh."

He was studying her seriously. "It didn't sound like a joke." He pushed his empty plate forward and leaned his elbows on the table. "Tell me more about how you fit into your family."

"For heaven's sake, I wish I'd never brought it up."

"But you did, Gayle, so finish it out."

"Oh, all right!" She pushed her plate aside and cradled her glass in her hands, looking down into the amber wine. "My dad petted and pampered and showed off my sisters, because they looked like little Dresden dolls. But he was embarrassed about me, because I looked like an ungainly carrot-topped colt as a child—and still do. Which would have been fine with him if I'd been a boy, but—"

"Not with me, it wouldn't," Cass broke in. "You're one of the—no, I'll take it one step farther. You're *the* most spectacular woman I've ever seen."

"For heaven's sake, I know you don't mean that! I can't stand it when people try to be kind!"

"Kind! You think I'm being kind? Believe me, Stormy, when it comes to my love life, I'm not into charity."

Gayle glanced up, puzzled by the intense tone in Cass's voice. The expression in his face spurred her heart into a gallop. His eyes were heavy as they touched the hair caught up on her head, then traced the shape and features of her face. His gaze lingered on her lips so long, they began to feel swollen with a memory of his kiss. Flares of response prickled the skin of her neck.

She gasped when his gaze moved slowly downward to caress her breasts. Her nipples tightened against the peachy drape of her blouse. The sensation was as explosive as one of his skyrockets, and rushed straight to the low, soft core of her body. She shivered over an ache of raw desire.

Cass smiled with soft, parted lips. He leaned forward and touched her lips with a finger. "You're no flamingo. I'm not sure what a bird of paradise looks like, but that's a name that fits you a lot better. You're exotically beautiful, Gayle. Tall and graceful and regal. The fanciest swan would look frumpy and ordinary beside you."

She wanted so badly to believe he meant what he said, but it had to be outrageous flattery. Still, it didn't seem possible for even Cass to fabricate an expression like the one on his face. He looked . . . bedazzled.

He ran the tip of his finger along her lip, from one corner of her mouth to the other. "Are you still hungry?" he whispered.

Staring at him blankly, she curled her fingers around his finger, holding it against her mouth. "Hungry . . . ?"

A smile curved his lips and lit his eyes. "Are you finished with dinner?"

It didn't matter that Gayle couldn't comprehend anything Cass was saying; he read an answer that pleased him in her eyes. "Why don't we go home before the pickup turns back into a pumpkin?"

"Yes, home." She kissed his fingertip and laughed softly. The memories were about to begin.

He buckled Gayle into the middle seat belt of the pickup, so that she was sitting against his side. Not even Cass had much to say on the way back. But he kept one arm over the top of the seat, sometimes touching her hair, sometimes her shoulder, or curling his hand around her neck.

Waiting for a light to turn green on the outskirts of town, he let go of the wheel and picked up her hand, placing it on his thigh, only inches away from that area of his body that so engrossed her. The energy coursing through the solid flesh under her fingers sang a love song. He glanced at her, his eyes lost in shadows. "Which home should I take you to?"

The unspoken question behind the question speeded her breathing. She tucked her fingers farther around his thigh and said soberly, "I don't know, but the house I'm living in isn't really a home."

"I actually had my castle in mind anyway," he said, outlining the whorls of her ear with his fingertip.

The light turned green, but he let the truck idle, since there were no cars behind them. "So, is that where you want to go?"

Shivering with a mix of excitement and apprehension, she said, "Well, if Cinderella had gone with her prince instead of running away, she wouldn't have had all those problems with shoes and . . . wicked stepsisters. Now that's something to ponder." She looked up into his face, smiling.

Cass grinned and exaggerated his drawl: "Before you go ahead and commit yourself to . . . whatever, I feel obligated to remind you that you're dealing with a coachman who might turn back into a rat at any moment, not a prince."

"There is that point." She nodded solemnly, took a deep breath, then made the leap; her voice sounded erotically husky when she said, "Your place it is."

"Yea-ah." Cass turned toward his side of the valley.

Eight

Moonlight gleamed on the silvery streaks in Cass's hair as he walked around the front of the pickup. After he'd handed Gayle down, she stood still, hugging her body to calm shivers of anxious excitement.

The night air seemed to quiver with expectation. Seductive earthy scents teased her nose. Leaves rustled, water babbled. An owl hooted, another answered hoo-*hoo* from the distance. It was a symphony of love sounds. Huge diamond stars glimmered in the black velvet sky.

"I didn't realize it could be so beautiful in the country," she whispered.

"It never was until you came along." The sound of Cass's deep voice intensified the magic. Taking her into his arms, he buried his face in her hair. "You don't know how badly I've wanted to hold you like this, sweetheart. Ever since the picnic. Ever since the first minute I saw you."

She curled her arms around his neck, pulling him closer. "I've wanted it too."

He smiled down at her, his heart beating against her, rapid and strong. "If you wanted to be in my arms as bad as I wanted to be in yours, it seems too miraculous to believe." Crushing her closer, he moved his lips tenderly over her eyes, her nose, her cheeks, her neck. "What else do you want, sweetheart?"

"I want . . . everything, I guess."

He grazed her lips with his, nibbled teasingly. "That sounded pretty vague, Stormy. Let's see if we can't pinpoint exactly what it is you're thinking about." He became more demanding. Forcing entry into her mouth, he ran his tongue in an agonizing line of fire along the inner surface of her lips. Then he drove deeper, giving her a foretaste of the greater moment.

"Tell me what you want," he whispered, thrusting his thigh between her legs.

She gasped, only able to stare back at him in the dark, too breathless over the sensations she was feeling to speak.

"What do you want?" he demanded, slowly moving his thigh against her. "Say it!"

"I want you, Cass."

Laughing softly, he stepped back and lifted her hand to his lips, touching it with his tongue. "That's my Stormy."

In the house he pressed buttons in the entry. Muted lighting came on in the peak-ceiling living room, romantic music murmured. His eyes were heavy and hot as he took her hand and led her down the hall.

A rash of goose bumps tightened her skin when they stood in the door to his bedroom. He touched a switch, and a small lamp came on, barely enough rosy light to push back the shadows. His oversize bed was neatly made up with a feather coverlet and pillows so puffy, they looked obscene. She stiffened with nervousness despite her desire and her intentions.

He smiled. "Surely, my bed can't make you feel so strange, sweetheart. You've seen it before."

She managed a crooked smile. "It's not your bed I feel strange about, it's . . ." She couldn't say it.

Cass took both her hands and walked backward, drawing her across the room. When they reached the bed, he whipped back the covers and grinned a challenge. "If you're having second thoughts, you'd better run now. This is the moment of truth. Leave or stay."

Gayle looked at the crisp, clean sheets and gave a brittle laugh. "Were you so sure of me that you changed your bed?"

"Not sure, just hopeful. I've been sweating bullets all evening, not knowing what you might decide." He made a face. "I still am, since you're hanging back like this."

She laughed. "I decided early on too. I'm going to stay, but . . ."

"This is no time for buts." He grinned and mimed a striptease with his jacket, tossing it on a chair. "It's time to say a brave yes or no, before things go too far." He sent his tie flying after the jacket and unbuttoned his shirt, pulling the tails out of his belt.

She stared at the brown hair curling on his heavily muscled chest. "I want to stay, I really do," she said, her voice full of emotion. Stepping forward, she ran her hands over his shoulders, which were awesomely broad under the pale yellow shirt.

He cupped a huge, callused hand on either side of her face, gently brushing her lips with his thumbs. "First time you were here in my bedroom I was so weak, you threw me around like a baby. The second time you were terrified of what I might do to you." His teasing smile turned soft with desire. "This time I'm in charge. Are you game to find out I'm not so terrifying after all?"

Her lips parted and curved under his thumbs. "Yes, Cass, I want that—I already know you aren't." She put her hands flat against his chest, against the nipples nestled in the hair.

"Yes, touch me . . . oh, you don't know what you do to me," he whispered, grazing trembling hands over the long, fair column of her neck. He slipped a finger down over the creamy, freckled skin in the deep V neck of her blouse, then cupped his hands under her breasts. "You're so lovely, sweetheart, so beautiful."

The instant he said "beautiful," she froze. She wanted so badly to be as lovely as he said, but she knew she wasn't.

Her nervousness turned into paralyzing shyness when he undid the buttons of her blouse. She pinched her eyes shut when he slipped her blouse off her shoulders and let it drop to the floor. She felt his fingers against her skin, unclipping the snap at the front of her lacy bra, brushing the sides apart, drawing circles on her rigid nipples with his thumbs. But not even the incredible sensation of his mouth on her nipple could thaw her.

"Darling . . . please," he whispered urgently. "I want you so much, hurry and get ready for me, please." His lips were swollen with desire when he kissed her mouth. His hands shook, fumbling at her zipper.

When he began pushing her skirt and slip over her hips, she whispered plaintively, "Aren't you going to turn the light out?"

"Oh, no, sweetheart, I want to see you."

No matter how badly she wanted him, even with the thrilling sweetness of his lips on hers, Gayle went rigid, every muscle tensed and shaking.

Cass stopped with her skirt midhip. He opened his eyes to look into hers, his lips going still on her mouth, his breath rasping in and out. He didn't move for a few seconds, just frowned into her eyes. Then his brows shot up. "Oh, hell, you're a virgin, aren't you, Stormy?" he whispered against her lips. "Why didn't you tell me, sweetheart?"

She pulled away from him with a strangled cry and splayed her hands over the blush rushing into her face. "I thought you'd laugh."

"Laugh! What kind of bastard do you think I am?" Cass scrubbed his hands over his face and took deep breaths, grappling with his galloping hunger. Then he said softly, "Gayle, I was bound to guess sooner or later, so you might as well have told me early on. I would have approached everything differently."

Swooping down to grab her blouse off the floor, she draped part of it over her breasts and buried her face in the rest. "Oh, I'm so embarrassed! I wish I were dead."

He stepped forward and took her wrists, gently pulling her hands and the blouse away from her face. "Why in the devil are you embarrassed? I thought you told me you knew all about naked men in bed."

"I do know all about *sick* naked men!" she cried, trying to jerk her wrists free. "But right now I'm not a nurse! I'm the only woman in the world who's made it to the age of *twenty-four* without knowing a damn thing about a naked man in . . . *my* bed. It's absolutely mortifying!"

"You little ninny," he said softly, letting her wrists go free. "Hell, you saw everything I've got a long time ago, so what's the big deal?"

"I'm not embarrassed about looking at you, it's—" She broke off and grimaced. "I'm embarrassed because I'm acting like such a stereotypical *virgin*. I honestly did mean to go through with this. I wanted to . . . I still want to. I still will. If you'd turn off the damned light, we can go ahead and at least take care of your little problem." She glanced down at the erection pressing against his fly. "Big problem."

Cupping his hand under her chin, Cass forced her to look him in the eye. "Do you actually think I'm the kind of guy who'd use you for my own gratification!"

"I didn't mean it like that!" Her face crumpled, and she dashed her balled blouse at the tears starting in her eyes. "Oh, all I wanted to do was build a memory to cherish. How could everything have turned into such a mess?"

"Ah, honey, I'm sorry."

"I don't want you to feel sorry for me."

"Look, why don't we have another go at it? I'll bet we can still build some spectacular memories for you."

"Cass Starbaugh, the last think I need is sexual charity from you!" Jerking up her skirt, Gayle hugged her blouse to her chest and fled from the bedroom.

"You total jerk!" Cass muttered over and over, while he cooled himself down and buttoned his shirt again. How could he have missed guessing the *pivotal* piece to the puzzle of his Stormy?

He hurried down the hall toward the living room with a doomed feeling that she'd be gone, walking home so she wouldn't have to look at his face again. He went weak with relief when he saw her staring out the window. Her clothes were back in order, and her hair looked dark in the dim light, as if he'd extinguished her fire with his stupidity. He desperately wanted her to trust him again, so he had to go at the touchy situation slowly and carefully—and watch his damned, undisciplined tongue for a change.

"Would you like some brandy?" he asked, walking into the room.

"No," she said, planting her back firmly toward him.

He stopped by the sofa. "Come sit down for a while."

"I don't want to sit down."

"Okay, that's fine. That's cool." When Cass crossed the room to stand near her, she stiffened. "Don't worry, I'm not going to pressure you into anything." He shoved his hands in his pockets. "You'll feel better if we talk about this."

"I'm never going to feel better again—ever." Her face, reflected in the window, looked droopy as a thirsty flower, paler than usual, making her freckles stand out. Her remarkable gray eyes looked huge.

"I'm so sorry, Gayle."

"Why should you be sorry?" she asked him.

"Because this should have been the most special night of your life." He wanted to beat his head against the wall when he saw her chin quiver. "Because everything about you should have told me you weren't experienced, but I was too dumb to see it."

"I really wish we could quit talking about it, Cass," she said, wrapping her arms around her body.

He raked his fingers through his hair. "I just want you to know that if I'd realized, I wouldn't have come after you like a damn bull in heat."

To his surprise she smiled, though she bit her lip to cover it. It was a hopeful sign that she could find something funny about the situation.

"Bulls don't go into heat," she said.

"You know what I mean."

She glanced at him for the first time. "I suspect I was the one in heat, riling the bull up."

"Were you in heat, Stormy? Then it's even more pathetic that I didn't make it good for you." He thrust his hands into his pockets. "Would you like that brandy now?"

"Yes, maybe I would."

He went to the liquor cabinet and poured a couple of ounces into each of two small crystal snifters, then gestured at the sofa. "Ready to sit down yet?"

"No."

"Okay." He came back and handed her a glass, watching her reflection in the window as she grimaced over a swallow.

"Look," he said after a moment. "I think I understand what you must have been feeling when you tensed up back there. I know I'm a big guy, and when my . . . well . . . certain parts of me get heated up, I expect I can be pretty intimidating to a woman on her first time." He twisted his lips and shrugged. "I just want to say that I do know how to be careful when I'm making love. I'd never hurt you, ever."

Gayle stared at him with wide eyes. "Is *that* what you thought?" She clasped her fingers around her wrist. "Cass, I wasn't afraid of *you*!"

"You weren't?"

"Oh, no, you're absolutely—" She broke off. "Well, size-wise, I suspect we're perfectly matched."

He lifted his brows, puzzled. "So what was your problem?"

She ducked her head and blew out a breath. "I went shy because I didn't want you to see *me* naked. I don't know why. Maybe because we were talking about the way my father acted with my sisters and me. All my old feelings of inadequacy must have come back up to the surface full force."

Cass put his hand over hers on his arm. "There's nothing inadequate about you, sweetheart."

"Sure, I'm adequate enough, but not—" She looked down at the huge hand covering hers. "All I could think of when you were taking my clothes off was that you've probably undressed *hundreds* of really beautiful women. I couldn't bear for you to compare me with—" She broke off and glared at him. "Cass Starbaugh, you stop laughing at me!"

He sucked in his cheeks to keep from grinning. "Hundreds of women? It exhausts me to imagine it." He couldn't hold back a chuckle.

"You're going to be more than exhausted, you're going to be a bloody pulp if you don't quit laughing." Gayle gave him a knuckle rap on the biceps. Her playful touch ran through Cass like an electrical current.

Setting his snifter on the windowsill, he put his arms around her from the back and breathed a sigh of relief when she didn't pull away. The softly draped material of her blouse felt alive against his hands, a silky caress in itself.

After a few moments he said, "Stormy, when I was sixteen, one of my sort-of uncles told me never to make love to a woman I wouldn't want to marry in a pinch. I took his advice to heart, and I've never made love to more than one woman I really liked at a time. And always in a nice, friendly relationship. How could there be hundreds of those along the way?"

"That's not what the people in town think."

He caught her eye in the window reflection and said very seriously, "I'm trusting you to keep all this in the strictest confidence. It would be a terrible thing to have the news nosed around that my reputation is all show."

She snorted a laugh. "Good Lord, yes! Governments have been known to crumble when lesser secrets got out."

Cass grinned. Bending his head, he kissed the creamy skin at the nape of her neck and felt her shiver at the touch. "I think what I'm trying to say is that I'm not always so wild as I was tonight. It's just that when I saw you in my bedroom, my brain clicked off, and Mr. Gusto took over." He moved his pelvis against her rear.

"Mr. Gusto!" she exclaimed, laughing.

"Yea-ah, I can hardly wait for you two to meet." He laid his face against her fiery hair. "He was a little overeager because I haven't made love since I met you."

Gayle examined his reflection with narrowed eyes. "Are you making that up?"

"No, I could swear an oath on it. Once I saw you, no one else looked interesting."

She turned around within the circle of his arms to face him. "But why me, Cass?"

"Why? Because ever since I met you, I've been thinking about you all day and dreaming about you at night. You've made my life miserable. You're a funny, fascinating person. And with that blazing hair of yours and those incredible eyes—even those damn freckles—you're absolutely, uniquely beautiful. You make all the other women look like a bunch of artificial Barbi dolls, that's why. And because I want to make love to you so badly, I think I might explode."

He nodded solemnly and moved his head forward to touch his lips to her mouth. "Besides, you're tall enough so I don't get a crick in my neck when I kiss you."

"Oh, Cass, you're such an idiot," she whispered. Slipping out of his arms, she distractedly paced around the room, looking at the bird paintings and Wild West prints. She read a few titles from the books on the shelves and studied his lighted mineral collection.

Cass followed her around the room like a lovesick puppy, cursing himself for his flip tongue. *A crick in the neck*, for the love of mud! No wonder she'd run scared from his lovemaking. It was a miracle she wasn't laughing in his face. When would he ever learn to watch his mouth?

Gayle wandered around the room, letting herself become accustomed to the new, amazing confidence she felt, now that she'd finally accepted the fact that Cass saw her as truly attractive. No idle flatterer would ruin his art with a spontaneous, sweet, idiotic comment about a crick in the neck. She'd seen her own beauty in his eyes, and she'd seen something more there too. Love.

She felt as if she were floating on the tender strains of the romantic background music. She felt weightless, as if he'd freed her from an anchor that had tied her down all her life. When she lit on the gray leather sofa, she felt as if she had to hang on or drift away.

It didn't help matters when he dropped down beside her and leaned his head on the sofa back, as if dejected. The lemony scent of his after-shave and the musk of his maleness sent her over the edge. "I want you to make love to me, Cass," she whispered.

He snapped his head up. "But I thought—" He studied her face with befuddled eyes. "Well, when?"

Laughing, she moved closer, running her hand up his thigh and over his fly. "Now, if Mr. Gusto is interested."

"Oh, my, is he!" he said with a gasp, pressing her hand in place. "But are you sure? I don't want any of this get-it-over-with business. I won't make love to you until you feel comfortable enough with me to strip down to your bare hide without blushing."

She lifted her head and looked around at all the big windows. "I don't think I'm ready to strip in front of the whole valley, but why don't we go back to your bedroom and see what happens?"

There was a delicious sense of expectancy about the house as Gayle walked hand in hand with him down the hallway. When they stopped beside the bed in the shadowy, rosy light, Cass smiled and put his hands on either side of her face. "Did you know you look beautiful in that peachy-pink dress of yours? As delicate as the inside of a pearly seashell."

"I never knew it before," she whispered, melting under his gaze.

"Well, you do." He kissed her gently, tenderly, then touched his tongue to her lips. She gave him entry, and gasped when he probed her mouth and jousted with her tongue.

The desire he'd kindled in his earlier kiss had been lurking just beneath her surface, and sprang up like a rapacious beast. A memory of his tongue on her nipples sprang up with it. She wanted that again, ached for the feeling. "Please, Cass, I want . . ."

His breath rasped when he lifted his head and looked questioningly down at her. "Show me what you want, Stormy," he whispered.

She hesitated only a moment, then unbuttoned her skirt and let it drop around her feet. She unbuttoned her blouse and let that fall, too, watching his face. The awe in his expression filled her with joy. Her breath exploded in short gasps when he touched the creamy, freckled skin between her breasts.

Wanting more, she unclipped her bra and shrugged it off. She closed her eyes in a mixture of strangeness, wonder, and joy when Cass cradled her breasts. He laughed softly. "Open your eyes and look at them, Stormy. See how perfectly they fit in my hands. They were created for love. For me."

She stared at his face, then looked down at his strong fingers, filled with globes of tan-flecked alabaster. She gasped when he rubbed his thumbs on her pink nipples, turning them as rigid as marbles.

"Do you like that?" he asked, his eyes on her face. "Tell me how it feels."

Her breath was coming so quickly, she could barely speak. "It feels like wires are tugging from your fingers right to the bottom of my body. Yes, I like it—yes."

He bent his head and took a nipple in his mouth, suckling, then turned his attention to the other. "Oh!" she cried out, as an agony of sensations flared through her body. "Oh, Cass! Yes, oh yes."

He lifted his head and grinned devilishly at her. "I believe you're blushing, Stormy. Are you going shy on me again?"

"I'm not blushing, I'm flushed," she cried, writhing under the sensation of his thumbs on her wet nipples. "I've never felt like this before."

He stepped forward and slid his thigh between her legs, rocking against her. "What do you want, Stormy?"

She grasped his arms. "You, Cass! I want you."

"You'll have to undress me to have me."

Gayle gave a throaty laugh, wanting nothing more than to see him in all his magnificence. Fumbling his buttons open, she pushed his shirt off his shoulders and down his arms. His skin was satiny under her hands. She gazed at his broad chest, ran her hand lightly only the curly hair.

She tongued his nipples, wanting to give him as much pleasure as he'd shown her. He shivered, and his breath came in gasps. Running her hands down over the magnificent, layered muscles of his stomach and sides, she laughed softly. "You're blushing, Cass."

"You're enough to flush a boulder." He groaned, restraining himself, with his arms held rigidly by his sides.

When Gayle touched his belt buckle, eager to see

the rest of him, he caught her hands. "Better wait a bit with that, I'm trying to hold back, but oh, baby, I'm starting to want you pretty bad. Besides, it's my turn." He slipped his fingers under her slip band and hesitated, his gaze meeting hers. "Ready?"

"Ready." First she fastened her gaze on his face, then looked down instead, watching his tanned hands slide over the creamy skin of her hips until her slip dropped. She pushed her own panty hose and shoes off.

In the shadowy light she watched him touch the lacy white triangle of her string bikini, felt him cup his hand under her. She gasped when he slipped his finger inside the lace. "Oh, Cass, oh, please."

"Please what?" he murmured, probing.

"Please, I want you," she cried.

He picked her up in his arms effortlessly and placed her on the bed. Bracing one knee beside her he leaned forward to ravish her mouth with his tongue. Gayle clutched him, winding her arms around his neck, arching her body toward him.

Lifting his head, his eyes hot and heavy, he grinned at her. "Think you're ready, sweetheart?"

She tangled her fingers in his hair and laughed softly. "If I get any readier, I'll expire. Will you quit dragging your heels and come in bed with me! What happened to that bull in heat?"

"I'm trying to civilize him." Cass stood on first one foot, then the other, taking his shoes and socks off. Then he unbuckled his belt. Watching Gayle's face, he pushed his slacks and shorts off. "This is it, sweetheart, the moment of truth. Yes or no?"

Gayle looked slowly down his awesome body. Smiling, she held out her arms.

He grinned. "I've got to take care of something first, so we don't end up with any inconvenient surprises."

"I took care of that before I left home."

"Oh, did you now?" Cass stretched himself out beside her, braced up on one elbow. "You mean to say you put me through all that worry and suspense about whether you would or wouldn't, when you started out with your decision made?"

Gayle laughed softly. "I didn't mean to put you through anything, but with an ego like yours, I doubt that it did you any harm." She ran her fingertips down his chest, over his stomach, and tenderly up his satiny, throbbing shaft. "Am I worth all the trouble?"

"Oh, baby, oh, Stormy." Cass shuddered in his effort to hold back. His hands were trembling as he pulled off her panties. Shifting around, he kissed the puff of fiery hair at the apex of her legs. With magic fingers he caressed her until she cried out for him. "Now, Cass, do it now."

Lifting himself onto her, he supported his weight on his elbows so he could look down into her face as he fitted himself against her. "It'll hurt a little, I'll try to be quick."

"I'm ready." She stared into his eyes and clenched her teeth against a cry when he entered. The pain ebbed when he lay still, filling her, one with her.

"You okay?"

She smiled up at him and took his face in her hands. "I've never been so all right in my life."

Pulling him down, she opened her mouth to his kiss. When she fenced with his tongue, he forgot himself and began moving inside her, whispering mindless love words with each stroke. "Stormy, sweetheart, oh . . ."

At first it only felt odd. Then a pressure seemed to come from inside her, turning his strokes into a delicious torment. The pressure mounted until the volcano seemed about to erupt.

"Oh, baby. Oh, Gayle, oh, Stormy . . . I can't hold

back any longer, I—" Cass convulsed against her, then collapsed, gasping hoarsely for breath.

She put her arms around him, kissing his sweaty neck and cheek, awed that she had given him so much pleasure. But her pressure ebbed slowly in a frustrating, disappointing way, as if a balloon blown up too tight had sprung a slow leak.

"You didn't reach a climax did you?" Cass whispered against her neck, when he had his breath back.

"Well . . . I felt lots of interesting things."

He groaned. "I'm not doing very well tonight. Now I've got two strikes against me."

Gayle petted his hair, loving the feel of him against her. "It's not you, silly. No woman can expect fireworks the first time."

Propping himself up on his elbows, he grinned down into her face. "There's nothing I like better than a challenge."

She laughed. "Maybe, but from what I can feel down there, Mr. Gusto isn't up to it."

"Boy, do you have a lot to learn, Stormy."

Cass lifted himself off and lay on his side, a knee holding her legs apart, lips over hers. His tongue stroked in and out. His magic fingers stroked in and out, too, bringing the volcano back to life, tormenting her until she moaned against his mouth. "What do you want?" he whispered.

Gayle writhed under his fingers. "I don't know—anything. Oh-h-h."

"Good, because Mr. Gusto has recovered.

She was so frantic, she barely noticed the pain when he slid himself into her again.

"Oh, Cass, oh, Cass," she cried, when he began moving relentlessly, first slowly, then, as he became excited, harder and faster.

She clawed him and screamed when the eruption

blew. Uncontrollable rapturous shudders racked her body. Vaguely, she was aware of Cass crying out and arching his back.

They lay together, gasping, sweaty. Slowly, she came back down to reality. "I had no idea it could be like that," she whispered wonderingly.

He lifted himself to the side and gathered her into his arms. "Think it lives up to all the hoopla?"

"*Does it!* You made it absolutely spectacular, darling."

He studied her face as if she were an unexpected, rare treasure. "That's the first time you've called me darling."

Gayle put her arms around his neck and smiled lazily. "I've thought it lots of times, but I've never been sure of you before. I am now."

"I'm glad." He brushed back the sweaty copper ringlets coiled around her face and kissed her forehead. "I was beginning to think you never would trust me."

"Darling," she said, trying out the feel and sound of it. "Darling, darling, darling Cass."

Sated and silent, they lay with their foreheads together, listening to the soft music. After a few minutes he said, "You're an attractive, desirable woman. You must have had boyfriends. Why'd you wait until now?"

She curled one long leg around his longer one and stretched her arm across his broad chest. "Sure, I had boyfriends, but none I cared enough about to bare all for. You're pretty special, and you make me feel special too. That's why you."

Cass gazed at her. "I'm not special, just very, very fortunate." He sighed deeply and ran the tip of a finger over the swell of her breast. He smiled. "Fairy kisses."

"What?" she murmured happily.

"That's what freckles are, fairy kisses." He ran his finger from her breast down the curve of her waist, up over her hip, and as far as he could reach on her leg. "Can you imagine fairies fluttering all over your body, kissing you—everywhere? Now that'd be a sight to behold."

She laughed. "What a titillating thought. Do you by any chance have a dirty mind?"

"You bet your sweet patootie I do." He gave her freckled rear a gentle slap.

"Watch it, buddy." She tweaked a chest hair.

They lay quietly for a few moments. "Stormy?"

"Mmm-hmmm?" She was twirling one of his straight, sun-bleached locks around her finger.

"It's not working."

"What's not?"

"Familiarity isn't breeding contempt, like they always say." Cass touched her full, sensual lower lip and gazed at her with limpid brown eyes.

"I can't say I find you very contemptible either." She laughed softly and kissed his nose.

"Now what in hell are we going to do about that?"

"Tell you what I'm going to do about it," Gayle said, sitting up. "I'm going home before I fall asleep here."

He ran his hand up her arm and teased her to lie back down. "Stay, there's plenty of room for two to sleep in this bed. Why run off?"

She got up and skipped out of range. "You know perfectly well why not. Half the people in the valley probably have telescopes permanently aimed at your house to see who sneaks out in the morning."

"Who cares what anyone thinks?"

"I do," she said, pulling her panties on. "We shared a magical time tonight, darling. I couldn't bear to hear everyone gossiping about it."

He smiled. "Magical. Mmm-*hmmm*." Swinging his long legs over the side of the bed, he stood up and stretched his arms languorously toward the ceiling, then clasped his hands on his head. "I suppose you think I'm gonna drive you home?"

"Uh-huh, I do think so." She slowly scanned him: bare feet, long legs, and slender hips, his massive chest and shoulders, impudently handsome face. "If you're into challenges, I dare you to do it dressed like that."

She gave a shriek of laughter when he dropped his arms and made a claw-fingered grab for her. "You better watch it, Miz Stormy Gayle, or you'll get yours one of these days."

"I certainly hope so." Taking a deep sigh, she stepped into his arms and pressed her face into the curve of his shoulder.

Her life seemed very perfect, secure, and complete at that moment.

Nine

Gayle awoke at nine the next morning, Sunday, feeling sore but deliciously sated. For the first time she'd slept through the night without having a nightmare. She'd slept better than she had in a year. Stretching luxuriously, she pictured Cass as he had looked standing by the bed in all his nude glory. She wondered if he was sleeping yet, what he planned to do that day, when she would see him again.

Rolling out of bed, she set up coffee to drip and stepped out to get her morning paper. She gasped. "Oh, my gosh!"

The porch was covered with flowers: A bouquet of long-stemmed red roses in a glass vase, another of lavender and white gladiola, a bunch of yellow jonquils, and a pot of lovely pink tulips. She stepped forward and picked an envelope off the roses. The card read, *To a joyous first, and many happy returns. Glad you waited.*

"Oh, Cass, you nut, so am I," she whispered, tears brimming over in her eyes. "Oh, so am I."

Wiping her cheeks, she brought the flowers inside and arranged them just so around the living room.

For the first time the little house took on a look of coziness and beauty. She ran to the phone and dialed Cass, but he didn't answer.

Restless, she slipped into pale green cords and a bulky knit beige sweater that hung low over her hips. Fixing her hair and face, she saw a new woman in the mirror, one with a radiant, smiling face. "I like you a heck of a lot better than the old one," she said, laughing softly. "I wish I'd known a long time ago that you're fairy-kissed, not spotty."

She fruitlessly tried calling Cass every fifteen minutes, and by twelve she still hadn't made contact. In between she wandered around the house in a daze, incapable of directing her attention to any of her remodeling projects. Shortly after noon she heard a knock. A blooming smile lit her face. Running to the entry, she yanked the door open.

But it was Bonnie on the doorstep, bright and chipper in tight jeans and a plaid cowgirl blouse. "I take it by the way your face dropped halfway to the floor, you were expecting someone else," she said, head cocked. "You said I should come have a look at your house. Is this a bad time?"

Gayle gave an abashed laugh and shook her head. "No, of course not. Come in."

Bonnie walked into the living room and stared at the flowers. "My, my *my*, spring has sprung for sure. I heard you went down Sula way to eat last night. That must have been *some* dinner."

Gayle quick-stepped to the roses and slipped the card into her pocket. "Where on earth did you hear that?"

"At church, from the Baxters. They happened to be there, too—said you and Cass made a handsome couple." Bonnie laughed when Gayle made an exasperated grimace. "You said you weren't after him, but it's beginning to look as if you've caught him. Or is it the other way around?"

Gayle shrugged apologetically. "There might be a little something going on. I'm sorry."

"Lord, girl, don't be sorry! Enjoy. As soon as I saw the two of you dancing at the Brass Rail, it was apparent you were made for each other. I've always felt like a Munchkin with Cass."

"You're not hurting, then?"

Bonnie smiled and shook her head. "No, I've known for years that much as I tried to make something out of it, Cass and I were never meant to be. I never could get anything more than a little kissing from him. He lived with my family for a year when we were kids, so I guess he saw us as brother and sister." Her eyes sparkled. "Besides, now I've got someone else on my mind."

"Oh, have you?" Gayle waved at the old oak table in the dining room. "Sit down and tell me all about it. I'll get some coffee." When they were seated with mugs in front of them, she said, "Who is this someone else you have on your mind?"

"Jackson." Bonnie sipped, sighed, then said dreamily, "I've known him since I started first grade, but I always assumed there wasn't much to him, because he's so quiet. However, he took me home the other night to the tune of a blistering farewell. So now I'm beginning to suspect still waters may actually run as deep as they say. I can't figure out how he worked up nerve to ask me to dance, but I'm sure glad he did."

"I guess the time must have been right," Gayle said innocently, blessing Cass for pushing him into it.

"Whatever. At any rate, I intend to dip my toe in the still waters, and see if they're warm enough for a swim."

Gayle smiled, propping her chin on her fists. "Forget the toe, dive right in."

"If you're handing out advice like that, I'll bet I can guess how the flowers came about." Bonnie laughed, then sipped contemplatively from her mug. "Now that you and Cass have had a . . . um . . . meeting of minds, I don't suppose you'll be leaving town. You'll probably want to stay and live in this little old house of yours, won't you?"

The question took Gayle by surprise; she lifted her chin off her fists, furrowing her brow. Was there a future for her and Cass? He had a world to explore yet, and she had . . . "My entire life is on hold and waiting for me back in Portland," she said slowly. "It never occurred to me not to go back."

"Everyone in town is hoping you'll change your mind and stay." Bonnie's eyes twinkled. "I am, too, though I'd give my left foot for a chance to sell your house. My purse is flat, and I need the commission."

Gayle smiled. "Whatever I do, I'll have to sell the house. It's my mother's, and she needs the money. Why don't you look it over and tell me how to go about putting it on the market."

"I'd be glad to." The flighty girl turned into a businesswoman as Bonnie began pacing through each room of the house. "It might be difficult to sell," she said when she'd finished the tour. "A family with children or teenagers isn't likely to go for a house with the master bedroom up here on the main floor, and the other two bedrooms in the walkout basement. That cuts out ninety-nine percent of your market."

Gayle groaned. "I didn't bring you in here to tell me the house is unsalable! After all my heavy labor? And there's still so much to do. The kitchen needs to be remodeled, carpets and linoleum replaced. Grass and shrubs planted in the yard. Should I or shouldn't I go on with it?"

"Did you hear me say unsalable? This is a perfect retirement home, so definitely slave on. But hold off on planting the yard. I just happen to know of an elderly rancher and his wife who want to move into town. They've heard all about what you're doing here, and I think they're interested. They'd probably want to do the yard themselves, just to keep their fingers in farming."

"They're really interested? How wonderful!" Gayle paused a second, then added, "I guess." She looked at the freshly painted living room and disastrous kitchen, feeling oddly possessive. "I can't believe this! I've actually become attached to this horrid little house."

"Why not? You've put your heart and soul into it," Bonnie said, smiling. "Whenever you're ready, come on down to the office, and we'll sign some papers. But that's enough about business—are you going to the airshow?"

"What airshow?"

"Don't you read the papers? They're going to have all sorts of aerobatics and whatnot. It starts at two. Everyone's going to be there. I'm surprised Cass didn't invite you."

Gayle was, too—an airshow seemed right up his alley. "He didn't mention it."

Bonnie snorted. "Neither did Jackson ask me, so let's just go on out there and have a blast on our own."

"Okay, we'll show them."

At one forty-five Bonnie and Gayle arrived at the airport, which was nothing more than a hanger and some sheds with a three-hundred-sixty-degree view of the mountains. Several mares with gangly new colts at their sides were grazing in an adjoining field, up to their knees in pastel wildflowers. Several small planes were roped down on the apron, along with a Learjet, property of a Hollywood personality who owned a summer home in the valley.

People were swarming all around the bright red and blue biplanes brought in for the airshow. Farther back on the runway were several olive-drab World War II planes and another odd-looking plane with a top wing and a fat body.

Not only was the tiny parking area jammed, but cars were strung up and down the access road. Bonnie drove her car into a bumpy pasture that had been opened to handle the overflow. They got out and walked up the road toward the spectators. "Why, there's Cass's pickup—so he did come," Gayle said when they reached the parking lot. "I wonder why he didn't ask me."

Bonnie made a face. "Men! Who can understand what motivates the critters. Oh, look, there's Carla and the girls."

A group of single men were standing near the young women. Jackson was at the fringes watching Bonnie arrive, but there wasn't any sign of Cass. Nor was he with the married or older people.

Everyone called out greetings, to Gayle as well as to Bonnie, making it evident she'd been accepted into the community. The girls teased her about her grass fire. When they drifted on to other subjects, generally related to men, Bonnie laughed. "I can't leave Jackson standing by his lonesome with all you sex-crazed females around. I better go rile up the still waters."

The airshow began with the two biplanes putting on a synchronized flying demonstration to the tune of oohs and aahs from the audience. The planes were finishing with a grand flourish when Gayle caught sight of Cass coming out of one of the buildings. "Oh, my Lord! What *is* he up to?" she said to Bonnie and Jackson.

He was dressed in a fluorescent yellow flight suit with blinding orange stripes down the sides. An orange crash helmet was strapped to his head, and a parachute was fastened to his back, the harness binding his crotch. He was a head taller than any of his four companions, in similar outfits of different colors.

"Oh, what fun!" Bonnie cried. "They're going to put on a skydiving exhibition. I didn't realize Cass was still doing that."

"Skydiving! Oh, no." Gayle groaned, her stomach lurching as she watched him climb into the fat-bodied plane.

"Why? Does it bother you, him doing that?"

"Yes, it bothers me! He could be killed!"

Bonnie laughed. "Nah, not Cass. He's always jumped into the middle of things and popped up smelling of roses. I remember one time he rafted down the Bitterroot River when it was in spring flood. He got hung up on the pilings under the silver bridge and nearly drowned. A couple of vacationing marines just happened to be in the right place at the right time to rescue him. So you see, he leads a charmed life. Right, Jackson?"

He grinned and nodded.

"Well, his life didn't look very charmed the first time I saw him." The engines of the skydiver's plane fired up, one at a time. "What if his luck has run out?"

"He'll be all right, you wait and see. Won't he, Jackson?"

He nodded encouragingly, mutely acknowledging Gayle's anxiety.

The plane taxied down the runway, swung around, and revved up its engines. Gayle clapped her hands over her ears against the deafening roar as it swept past and was airborne. Banking to the east, it came around in a circle and began its run down the valley, climbing steeply.

Far to the south, it circled around and came back, flying so high it looked like a toy. Gayle clasped her hands, biting into a knuckle. Every muscle in her body was pulled tight. She couldn't bear to watch; she couldn't take her eyes off the approaching plane.

Just before it passed over the airport, the five men dropped out of the belly and plummeted downward, turning lazy synchronized somersaults. Joining hands, they formed a five-pointed star. When they separated, rainbow-color parachutes began blossoming.

Gayle forgot to breathe, staring at the vivid yellow-and-orange of Cass's suit. His parachute hadn't opened. Every broken, bloody body she'd ever seen ran through her mind. "Oh, God, please, *please* . . . let it open," she whispered against her knuckle.

She went weak with relief when multicolor silk finally streamed out behind him, bulging up into a rectangular hood. Dangling and swaying, he manipulated the parachute toward a big white X painted in the pasture. Landing on his feet, he ran with the momentum, then stopped and grabbed the strings to pull in the silk.

"See, didn't I tell you there was nothing to worry about?" Bonnie said.

Gayle pressed a cupped hand around her mouth and pinched her eyes tightly shut to prevent herself from losing control and howling.

Bonnie patted her on the shoulder. "Oh, come on, silly, if you're gonna hang around Cass, you'll have to get used to things like this. Right, Jackson?"

Gayle opened her eyes. His dark face was full of enough concern to induce him to vocalize. "Yup."

"I'll never get used to it. Never!" Clamping her teeth against chattering, she watched Cass join the other jumpers across the runway. They were unfastening their harnesses as they walked toward the hanger. "I've got to talk to him," she said, taking a wobbly step in his direction.

"Maybe that isn't the best idea in your state of mind," Bonnie said, catching her arm. "You wouldn't want to throw off his concentration just before he goes up again."

"He's going to do that *again*?"

"Probably—as soon as they put on new chutes. Right, Jackson?"

He had his head cocked, brows pulled down over his eyes. "Uh-huh."

Gayle watched, frozen, as the plane landed and taxied toward the hanger. Her stomach twisted into a knot. She was afraid she might embarrass herself by throwing up right there in front of everyone. "Bonnie, could you take me home? I can't watch any more of this."

"Oh, sure. No problem," her new friend said.

When she got home, Gayle threw herself on her bed and sobbed bitterly. Then she got up, washed her face with icy water, and began thinking—which was far worse than weeping. A picture of Cass plummeting out of the sky toward the earth replayed over and over in her mind.

She stood by the window, staring at the charcoal-gray storm clouds moving in from the pass at the south end of the valley.

Why on earth had she let herself fall in love with Cass Starbaugh, the most unsuitable man in the world for her? How could she have been so naive as to think heartbreak and regrets or heartbreak and beautiful memories were the only alternatives? She could survive those. But how could she survive the terror she'd felt this day? Was it going to happen again . . . and again? How could a man be so sweet one minute, and cause her so much confusion, horror and . . . yes . . . even anger, the next?

A familiar rat-a-tat knock startled her out of her brooding. Gayle hesitated for a moment, pressing her hands to her face, confused about what she wanted to say to Cass.

But the instant she opened the door and saw him, she melted. He looked stunning in a western shirt, a cowboy hat, boots, and a worried smile. Every emotion but love went on hold in her mind. "Hi, darling, I didn't expect to see you here."

He brushed her cheek with a knuckle. "I missed you."

She pulled him into a living room filled with scent and color. "Thanks for the morning-after flowers. It was so sweet and original of you." She wrapped her arms a little desperately around his neck.

He enfolded her into a full-bodied embrace. "Were you surprised?"

"I was so astonished, I nearly fainted. Where on earth did you find so many flowers in the middle of the night? Did you break into a florist's shop?"

He smiled, gazing down into her face with tender brown eyes. "Something like that. A sort-of cousin of mine owns a greenhouse. I did him some favors once, so I rousted him out of bed and called in my chit. I had to put up with some rather explicit grumbling, but he did it."

"Poor man, but I love them." She dug the card out of the pocket of her cords and smiled as she read it again. "After I found the flowers, I tried to call you and tell you I'm glad I waited, too, but you weren't home."

His smile wavered and faded. "Well . . . I had some things to do."

Her on-hold emotions reared their ugly heads again. Pulling out of his arms, Gayle touched one of the red roses and quietly forced the issue. "Things to do at the airshow?"

Lifting his hat, Cass ran his fingers through his hair, then settled it forward over his eyes. "It was a surprise to hear you'd dropped in over there."

"And I was a little surprised to see you there too," she said in a chilly voice. "I can still hear airplanes buzzing around, so I'm also surprised you left before the show ended."

Cass studied her face. "Jackson had a few things to report about how my jump affected you. He ended up by saying—and I quote—I'd better haul my stupid ass over here and straighten things out with you."

That surprised a laugh out of her. "Jackson said all that? I didn't think he ever talked."

"Sure, but unlike some people I could mention, he only talks when he has something important to say." He shoved his hands into his pockets. "I understand you saw me jump."

"Yes, I certainly did."

"What'd you think of it?"

"You looked very . . . colorful," Gayle said, turning to look out the window. The storm clouds were traveling down the valley toward town. "How did you happen to get into something like skydiving?"

He shrugged. "I thought it would be a thrill. And it is."

She stared at a pristine white thunderhead burgeoning out of the gray clouds, then glanced back at Cass. "Why did you wait so long after everyone else to open your parachute? I was terrified for you."

His brown eyes were defensive under his hatbrim. "No need to be, I had it all worked out. Split-second timing is the challenge."

"The challenge!" She shuddered. "But what if your timing had been off, and you'd opened your parachute too late? Or it hadn't opened at all? You would have been killed!" She rushed forward and buried her face in his shoulder.

"Sweetheart, I swear I knew what I was doing." He held her tightly, running a comforting hand over the long sweep of her back. Then he cupped his fingers under her chin and lifted her face. "It was probably more dangerous driving over here to see you than jumping. There aren't many drunks up in the sky."

"What a ridiculous rationale." Angry that he could joke about something so serious, Gayle pulled away and looked out the window again. Jagged spears of lightning were slicing down at the mountains from the vanguard clouds. Thunder rolled ominously. The airshow planes had retreated.

Gayle turned to face Cass. "Maybe I wouldn't have been so upset if you'd brought me to the airshow yourself and had told me what you were going to do. Maybe I could have prepared myself."

"I realize now that I should have." Brushing her feathered, coppery bangs up, he kissed her forehead. "But at the time I didn't think you knew about the airshow, and I thought I was protecting you." He pushed his mouth up in a wry grimace. "Besides, I wasn't too eager to hear what I was fairly certain you'd say about daredevil skydivers."

The room darkened as the clouds covered the sun. "So you do admit you're a daredevil," she said angrily.

He studied her face, waited out a flare of lightning and crackling blast of thunder. "You wouldn't be trying to entrap me into admitting guilt I don't feel, would you, Miz Stromm?" he asked in a deceptively soft drawl.

Hugging her anger in with arms wrapped around her body, Gayle said in an equally soft voice, "Maybe we'd better quit talking about this, or next thing we know I'll be asking you to settle down and quit risking your idiotic neck."

His eyes narrowed, and his chin came up sharply. "Gayle, I don't want to cause you anxiety, but I—"

She broke in, her voice rising. "Don't worry, Cass—I don't intend to ask you to change. I'm smart enough to know that'd be both useless and unfair."

There was as much confusion, anger, and yearning on his face as she felt. As if the conflict were pulling him apart too.

She tried to smile. "You tapped Cinderella with your magic wand and showed me I was a special woman after all. Now I'm finding out I can't cope with the ways of the prince. But I can't bear to sit in ashes again either."

His angry expression melted, and he came forward with his arms raised. "Ah, sweetheart, I—"

With a blue flash and a house-rattling explosion, lightning struck a tree in the field down below. Gayle jumped an inch and threw her arms around Cass. She strained against him desperately, her soul filled with a mix of love for him and terror that she might lose him again.

His hat fell off when she began scattering frantic kisses on his face. "Make love to me, darling! Please . . . right now."

The force of her desire shocked him into action. His hands found her breasts, then cupped her buttocks to pull her closer. His eyes turned heavy and hot, his lips softened under her kisses. "Are you sure, sweetheart?" he whispered.

"Yes, *yes*!"

Sinking to the carpeted floor, she pulled him down after her. They barely ripped their clothes out of the way before coming together, Cass on his back, Gayle straddling him. Lightning flashed, streak upon streak, thunder rumbled and crackled. The first sheets of driving rain slashed the window, drowning out her cry of climax. He arched with his release, groaning. "Sweetheart, yes . . . yes."

She pushed the sides of his unbuttoned shirt away and buried her face in the crisp, curly hair on his chest. He played his fingers in her tangled hair. They lay still, panting for several moments. The storm was passing, the thunder rumbling in the distance now.

Cass laughed softly, another rumble under her ear. "Now you know why I call you Stormy. You rivaled the fireworks, jolt for jolt."

She nuzzled his collar aside to kiss him on his neck. "You gave the lightning a run for its money yourself, smarty."

He held her close, both arms wrapped around her back. "You know something?"

"I know lots and lots. What do you know?"

"I've been thinking."

She propped her elbows against his shoulders and grinned down into his face. "I'm listening."

He touched her nose. "You'd better, because I've come to the conclusion that not a thrill in the world could compete with the thunder and lightning you just got done serving up to me."

Her smile ebbed. "What do you mean?"

His expression was loving, but there was something guarded and reluctant in his eyes. "I mean it isn't fair for me to cause you worry and pain. The daredevil stuff isn't that important."

Gayle stared at him, wondering why she wasn't eager to hear him say what she'd so wanted to hear earlier. She snapped her bra together in front and pulled down her bulky sweater. "Don't promise anything you don't really want to do, Cass."

He arched himself up on his heels to pull up his briefs, then struggled awkwardly to his feet with his jeans around his cowboy boots. "You're more important to me than any skydiving," he said, pulling up his jeans. "And I sure as hell had better rethink the barnstorming one of the pilots and I were talking about. He wanted me to stand on the wing while he did his acrobatics and—"

"Oh, my *God!*" Now, along with the image of Cass plummeting to earth with an unopened parachute, she pictured him clinging to the wing of a single-engine plane, hanging upside down in a barrel roll. "When are you going back to your mountain climbing? It's beginning to sound absolutely safe, compared to these other bizarre escapades."

He didn't answer, but his expression closed down so fast, she imagined she could hear the gates clanging shut. He began buttoning his shirt, avoiding her eyes.

She stared at him. "You *are* nervous about climbing since the accident, aren't you?"

"Just drop it, okay?" Cass jammed his shirttail into his jeans and zipped his fly. "I've made my decision—I care a hell of a lot more about you than I do about anything else." He tried for a light grin, but it came out looking like a grimace as he fastened his silver rodeo award belt buckle. "So . . . my two dives today were my swan song, sweetheart."

She studied him for a moment, then pulled her string panties on. "You make me feel like a ball and chain around your leg."

"You aren't forcing me out of anything. It's my decision, I swear." He drew an X over his heart. "From now on I'm Mr. Conservative."

Instead of relief or gratitude, Gayle felt an odd sense of bereavement, as if she were losing something. She pulled on her cords and walked across the room to look thoughtfully out the window. The storm had passed, and the clouds were breaking up. The rain had washed away the black of her grass fire, and the horses and Herefords were grazing on the bright green grass underneath. She pictured Cass foremost in the line of firemen, fighting the blaze.

Turning, she said, "The problem really isn't you and what you do, it's me and how I feel about trauma. But I'm going to be selfish and accept your sacrifice anyway. Only because I want so badly to be with you as much as possible during the short time we have left together. After I'm gone, you can go back to doing all the things you enjoy."

Cass stared at her, his dark brows lowering over his eyes. "What, exactly, are you telling me?"

Gayle glanced at him, wondering why he looked angry again. "I'm telling you that I love you, and I love having you make love to me. But we haven't made any promises. I think we both agreed there were no permanent relationships in the deal—right?" She waited, not sure what she wanted him to answer.

He rubbed his neck, gazing at her with a wistful scowl. "Right . . . I guess. But I don't want you to leave."

"I never planned to stay, Cass. The only reason I came to Hamilton was to get over my trauma burn-out. I'm not dreaming about blood and guts any longer, and my three-month leave of absence is up in a few weeks. So pretty soon it's back to Portland for me."

He stepped forward and grabbed her upper arms. "You sound as if you're already making plans. What about your house!"

Gayle gave him a shaky smile. "Bonnie thinks she has a buyer for it."

"Oh, damn Bonnie to hell!" He crushed her into his arms. After a moment he whispered, "Nothing seems to last forever, does it? Why is that?"

The sadness in Cass's voice cut through her heart. "I don't know," she answered, pressing her face into his neck. "But I don't suppose we were ever meant to be."

Ten

Harvey Fenster's condition had been deteriorating. He seemed even weaker by the middle of the next week. "Won't be long now, will it?" he said after Gayle had checked him over.

"I don't think so." Her voice was kind, but she felt frustrated and angry, because the only therapy either Harvey or his doctor would allow were comfort measures and her company. She was accustomed to Critical Care, where his illness would have been treated aggressively. "How do you feel about that?" she asked, taking his gnarled old hand in his.

"I'm ready—eighty years on this tough old earth are enough. And I sure as hell ain't a lot of good to myself the way I am now." He breathed heavily, adjusting the oxygen prongs in his nose, then changed the subject. "How's your house comin'?"

"Cass helped me redo the kitchen, and I hired a painter to spray the outside."

"I suppose you did it in pink or purple. I dunno why you damn outsiders have to come in and paint things funny colors—even the barns."

Gayle laughed. "I painted it the only color that was on sale. Which was white."

"Well, all right, I suppose that's sensible enough."

"Now all that's left to do is to buy new carpets and linoleum. And I think I've sold the house."

He peered at her, his white brows pulled down to hide the anxiety in his eyes. "You ain't leavin' before I pass over, are you?"

She pressed his hand. "I'll try my very best to be here, Harvey."

"I damn well hope so. Nothin' I hate worse than breakin' in a nurse, then have her run out on me." He grunted and changed the subject. "What's goin' on around town?"

"Big excitement! Jackson and Bonnie Breckenridge are getting married. Their friends are staging a to-do at Lake Como on Saturday to celebrate the engagement. I'm going with Cass."

"There something goin' on between you two too?"

She and Cass had slipped into an uneasy togetherness, making love, laughing, ignoring the passing days and the uncertain future. "Maybe a little something."

"'Bout time someone pinned that boy down." He wheezed a laugh.

She only smiled; he didn't need to know the joy wasn't forever.

"Neighbor of mine told me about the airshow," he said in another of his abrupt topic changes. "Once I wanted to learn how to fly an airplane—back when they first came out."

Gayle tried to imagine Harvey sitting in the open cockpit of a biplane, a pilot's cap and goggles on his head, a scarf whipping out behind him. "Why didn't you?" she asked, smiling.

"The lessons cost too much, and on top of that I was scared spitless." He wheezed for a minute, his brow creased in thought. "I heard you had the stuffin' scared out of you when Cass dropped out of the sky."

"Isn't *anything* sacred?" Gayle demanded, rolling her eyes toward the ceiling.

"Better get that boy back up on a mountain before he breaks his damn neck!" He squeezed her hand painfully hard, then went into a coughing fit. When it was over, he closed his eyes, too exhausted to continue.

"You rest now," Gayle said softly, and kissed him on the forehead, something she'd never done before.

His eyes popped open in surprise. He squeezed her hand again and muttered, "Damn redhead."

Gayle left him in the care of his attendant and drove back toward town, wondering why Harvey kept harping about Cass's mountain climbing.

By two on Sunday afternoon Gayle and Cass, along with a couple dozen other single and young married people, had eaten themselves silly at the mammoth potluck picnic meal. They'd toasted Jackson and Bonnie's engagement with talking, teasing, joking, laughter, and beer. Then everyone scattered to play softball, badminton, and volleyball. Four motorboats were launched, and several men who had wet suits took turns waterskiing.

Because their time together was growing so short, Gayle and Cass left the crowd to be by themselves. They stood on the earthern dam, looking out over the azure-blue lake. It was at its prime in May, so full the waves were almost lapping at their toes. The air was scented by the pine forests on the hills rolling down to its shores. Songbirds were courting in the trees. Far up in the sky a pair of eagles soared.

"Like it?" Cass asked, putting his hand over hers on the railing.

"It's gorgeous," she answered, though there was a severity about the beauty that made her uneasy.

The sun was intense enough to burn her to a crisp. Luckily, she'd had the foresight to put on jeans, a long-sleeve pale blue jersey, a floppy hat, and plenty of sunscreen to protect her delicate skin.

And all those mountains made her breath catch. The three snowcapped cones rising beyond the end of the lake were so tall, they seemed a direct link to all outer space. Perhaps that was what Cass meant when he'd said he felt like he owned the universe when he stood on top of a mountain. "Well, they still make me feel claustrophobic," she muttered.

When he didn't answer, she glanced at him. His big body, in a brown T-shirt, tan safari shorts, and canvas hiking boots, seemed at one with the rugged landscape. Without a cap his hair shone gold in the sun. It surprised her to see his lips turned down and his forehead furrowed. She couldn't tell if he was looking at the mountains or the waterskiers. "Do you wish you were skiing, darling?" she asked, choosing the lesser of two evils. "I won't hold you to your promise."

He came to life and took a deep breath. "No, because I don't have my wet suit, and that water is *cold*."

She couldn't leave the subject alone. "You looked so pensive just now—do you wish you were climbing the mountains?"

He shied away from a straight answer by drawling teasingly, "Nah, Stormy, I'm wishing I had you home in bed. Even with that hat, the fairies are kissing your freckles brighter and prettier by the minute, and I'm jealous."

She smiled, the look in his eyes melting her anxiety

away. "Aren't you a lovely man for saying so. But if you go around looking as gloomy as you just were, people might think you begrudge losing that Breckenridge girl to your partner."

"I do believe you're learning how things work in a small town." Leaning forward, he kissed her, pulling the brim of her hat around their faces. She twined her arms around his neck.

After a few moments he lifted his head and grinned. "There, now they can see I'm surviving the disappointment and holding up pretty well."

Gayle glanced down at the picnic site and realized they were in plain view of everyone. Backing out of his arms, she exclaimed, "You did that on purpose, you beast!"

"Beauty and the Beast," he agreed, laughing.

Gayle went sober again when she realized he still looked restless and moody. "Want to hike up the road and work off all the food?" she asked, hoping physical activity might distract him.

"Sure, but since you've got your hiking boots on, let's do the trail to the head of the lake instead."

She glanced at the three jagged mountains. A shivery premonition ran through her body. "Okay," she said, refusing to believe in forebodings.

When Gayle and Cass announced their intention to hike around the lake, several other people came along. With tomfoolery and high jinks, it took over an hour of trudging to reach their destination.

The lake was fed by a sizable stream catapulting from a needle's eye of a canyon. Cass took Gayle's hand, pulling her up onto the huge boulders above a series of cascades roaring down into the lake. Rainbows danced in the misty spray.

The others clambered up and swarmed around, laughing and shouting over the roar of water. "Hey, let's climb to the top of that," one of the men chal-

lenged, pointing at the granite wall rising some
twenty feet above the other side of the cascades.
Someone else yelled, "You're on!" And they made a
mad rush for the footbridge spanning the mouth of
the river. "Come on, Cass! You're the expert here, get
a move on. Last one up's a rotten egg."

Gayle glanced quickly at him, dreading his agreement. To her surprise he was frozen motionless,
staring at the men already swarming up the cliff.
Beads of sweat had broken out on his forehead and
upper lip. His eyes were pinched, his mouth twisted.
"Cass, what's wrong?" she asked, putting her hand
through his arm.

He started at the sound of her voice, and dragged
his gaze away from the wall. "Let's get out of here," he
said with a growl, and hustled her off the boulders.

Gayle's legs were long, but not long enough to
match his strides. "Slow down, where's the fire?"

He stopped and looked back at her. "Sorry."

She caught up and took his hands. "What happened back there, darling? What's wrong?"

"I don't want to talk about it." He pulled his hands
away and trudged more slowly down the woodsy
path, his back held as stiff as a crowbar. Farther on,
he stooped to pick up a stick and slashed at brush as
he walked.

Gayle followed silently, watching the play of power
in the muscles of his bare legs. She hadn't believed
Harvey when he'd suggested Cass was afraid to
climb. But she did now, after seeing him suffer a
virtual panic attack. She didn't know how to comfort
him or what to say.

When they got back to the picnic tables and boat
landing, Cass puttered around for a few minutes,
poking at things with his stick. "Maybe I *will* ski a
turn or two around the lake," he said finally.

The look on his face caused Gayle's heart to leap.

He wasn't just moody now—he was in a blue funk. Her sense of premonition intensified. "But you said you don't have a wet suit, and the water is freezing."

"I know, I know, but I must've skied here hundreds of times. I should be expert enough not to spend too much time in the water. And if I do, I'm not so sweet I'll melt."

She eyed his defiant grin. "You aren't in any mood to be racing around behind a speedboat."

He impatiently threw down the stick. "What's mood got to do with it?"

The tone of his voice was snappish, and Gayle responded resentfully. "It all depends on whether you're going out there to ski for fun or to prove something."

"Stormy, I told you before, you're the worst fuss-budget in the whole Northwest Territory." Whirling around, he stumped to the dock. Yanking his boots and socks off, he waded out into the lake to fit the skis onto his feet.

Gayle knew he was right—waterskiing wasn't a hazardous sport. But a full gamut of old trauma demons rose up to torment her as she watched the boat accelerate with a roar. Water sheeted off the rope as Cass was pulled upright. He flew away from her, his big frame gracefully balanced on the skis. Sun gleamed on the hair flying back from his forehead.

She ran along the shore and out onto the middle of the dam for an unobstructed view of the lake. Anxiety made her feel light-headed as she shaded her eyes against the glare, watching him. "Damn you, Star-baugh, you better be careful!" she muttered.

But it wasn't in Cass simply to skim over the water. He was maneuvering from side to side, bouncing over the fanning waves of the wash. Far down the lake the boat roared into a tight turn, swinging him out to the side, the wash pitching him up in great leaps.

To Gayle's mind the boat seemed to be speeding excessively as it headed back down the lake toward her. She prayed he'd be satisfied with one lap. When he was almost back at the landing, she allowed herself to breathe a sigh of relief.

But then another boat, going at an equally excessive speed with a skier behind, made an unexpected turn and cut in front of Cass's boat. His driver swerved to the side, whiplashing Cass toward shore.

She gave a choked cry when he tobogganed over a submerged boulder and went airborne. For a moment it seemed he would recoup and land on his skies. But then he lost it. His legs and arms pinwheeled, skis flying off. He landed among the boulders, sending up a geyser of water.

Gayle screamed. Her worst nightmare had come true.

It was dark when Cass came out of the emergency room with ten stitches in the laceration just above his left eyebrow. Shivering in the passenger side of Gayle's car, he still felt half-frozen, though he was wrapped in a borrowed hospital blanket. Worse, his Stormy wasn't talking to him. She'd refused to acknowledge his apology for putting her through such a worrisome ruckus, and that was scary.

She still didn't say anything as they walked into his house, she just hustled him down the hall. After running his shower up to hot, she broke the silence with a tart "Get in there and warm yourself up. You're still blue around the lips from that icy water."

Cass let her help him take his clothes off, then stepped into the hot spray. After she'd slammed out of the bathroom, he hit the tiled wall with both fists

and gave a bellow of frustration, thoroughly dis-
gusted with himself.

He'd warmed up by the time he came out into the
living room wearing a brown sweat suit and wool
socks. Gayle had built a fire in the fireplace, but the
atmosphere wasn't very cozy. Her hair was tousled
from the day outdoors, and as red as the flames. Her
expression was icy, as she sat on the sofa with her
arms wrapped around her body. He winced when he
saw that her turtleneck jersey and her jeans were
stained with his blood.

Pouring brandy into a couple of snifters, he
handed one to her in a conciliatory gesture. "Here,
drink this—you looked chilled too."

She set the glass on the coffee table and scowled at
the stitched wound on his forehead. "I'm not chilled,
Cass, I'm mad as hell!"

"Well, if you hadn't told me, I wouldn't need a
fortune-teller to guess." He gave a wry laugh and put
his brandy down too. "Okay, let's get it over with. Go
ahead and say you told me so. Tell me that was one of
the dumbest things I've ever done and that I'm an
idiot."

She glowered at him. "You said it, not me."

"I'm sorry. What else do you want me to say?"

"I want you to be open and honest about what you
feel for a change, and about why you got yourself into
this accident."

Now she was zeroing in on things he didn't like to
think about and sure as hell didn't want her to know.
He took a stand in front of the fire, legs spread, arms
folded. "I had a little skiing accident and ended up
with a bruise or two and a few stitches. Outside of a
headache and a few hundred muscle aches, I don't
feel anything about it. Is that honest enough for
you?"

She jumped up and squared herself off in front of

him. "You could have been killed!" she cried. "When you went flying and crashed into the rocks, every trauma patient I ever saw rose up from my memory in living, three-D color."

He winced. "Look, I realize you have a problem about those things, but—"

"*I've* got a problem? Cass, you *promised* me you wouldn't risk your neck while we're together!"

"Stormy, I've never considered waterskiing to be a particularly risky sport."

She gave him a scathing look with those light eyes of hers. "It isn't for anyone else! But you were in such a mood you went out of your way to make it dangerous."

"That's ridiculous! Why would I do such a thing?"

"That's exactly what we need to talk about! What *you* need to talk about. Why *do* you do things like that?"

"What's done is done, Gayle. Let's drop it, okay?" he said, jutting out his chin.

"No, let's not, because I think I know the answer. When I saw what you did today, I finally understood what Harvey has been trying to get across to me."

"How the hell did Harvey get into this conversation?" he demanded. "Didn't you learn your lesson when you took his advice and almost burned up those cows? If you're not careful, he'll have you fry us next."

"Harvey cares about you! Everyone cares about you," she said furiously. "But you go around teasing and joking to ward off everyone's honest concern."

"I suppose I must, if you say so." He unfolded his arms and balled his fists defensively by his sides. "But you're nosing around where you don't have any business, Gayle."

"I think I have a right to nose around, because I love you." Moving closer, she studied him, and must have seen everything he was trying to hide, because the anger faded out of her face. "You've been scared out of your wits about climbing since your accident, haven't you?"

Cass froze. He couldn't bring himself to admit he wanted to climb so badly he ached with the need but didn't have the courage. His fear made him feel less than a man—the last thing he wanted his Stormy to think. "I don't know what you're talking about."

She took one of his fists between her hands and uncurled his fingers. "I'm talking about how you actually broke out in a cold sweat when someone asked you to climb up that little cliff at the end of the lake. And then you immediately went and bashed yourself up."

He muttered a blue-tinged observation about her keen perceptions, and she dropped his hand and retreated. "I know why you're jumping out of planes and trying to be superman, Cass," she said, forging on. "You wouldn't be doing those things if you'd just get yourself back up on a mountain."

He yanked the jacket of his sweat suit down around his hips. "Well, if that isn't some damn three-hundred-sixty-degree turnaround. First day I met you, you made some big fuss that climbing was risking my neck for a cheap thrill."

Heat lightning flickered behind her gray eyes. "Boy, was I naive that day. Now that I've seen you plummet out of the sky and go ass-over-applecart showing off on a lake, climbing sounds like baby play. Get back up on that cliff, will you? Then maybe you can quit risking your neck to convince everyone you aren't a coward."

"Well, thank you for the analysis, Dr. Freud," Cass said sarcastically. Turning his back, he stared into the fire. For the first time in his life someone had seen through his teasing facade and ferreted out his inner feelings. It scared him to be so vulnerable. How could he go on living if he opened himself up to her and she deserted him anyway?

Gayle paced angrily around the living room, her breasts vibrating under the clinging material of her jersey. "I'm sorry if you don't like what I'm telling you, but that's how it looks to me," she said after a few moments. "And I love you too much to stand by without saying something while you risk your neck."

Cass knew everything she said was valid, despite how much he hated to admit it. And it was probably good for him to have the facts thrown in his face, but he just couldn't bring himself to give in. "If you love me all that much, then how come you're so eager to run back to Portland?"

"You know why I have to go."

"No, I don't. Tell me why."

"Well, because my whole life is there. My mother needs me. My job . . ." She looked bewildered, as if her reasons didn't stand up to scrutiny.

"Your mother's an adult—she can take care of herself. And how in hell can you go back to Critical Care nursing when you can't even tolerate a simple laceration? You're a fine one to be hitting on me about my phobias."

She put her hand around her turtleneck collar, as if he'd gone for her throat. "Where do *you* get off hitting on me about my problems and about my leaving? I haven't had any better offers to encourage me to stay."

Faced with a commitment, Cass felt almost as if he were cartwheeling over rocks again—in deep danger. To put himself in a position to love and lose was terrifying. "Huh! If I made an offer, I can't see you saying yes."

Snapping his mouth shut, he studied her, barely breathing, then ventured a cautious "*Would* you marry me? If I happened to ask."

She gazed at him with yearning written all over her face. Then she fixed her gaze on the stitches over his eyebrow and said in a low voice, "Please don't ask. . . . I don't know just now."

Just as he'd expected! A great emptiness was opening up inside him. All the love and happiness he'd shared with Gayle seemed to be cracking and falling away—like the glowing coals of the fire, which suddenly popped an explosion of sparks: He opened the screen and bleakly threw in another log. "I guess nothing we had together went deeper than the surface," he said miserably.

Her eyes looked so big and sad, they seemed to cover half her face. "It went deep for me! But you're so stubborn, you'd let your fear of climbing come between us."

"I'm stubborn! *Me*?" Cass dropped onto the sofa and ran his fingers through his hair.

After several silent minutes he clenched his jaw, then forced himself to say, "Okay—all right. If that's what you want, I'll climb Blodgett Canyon." He narrowed his eyes and studied her. "But only if you come with me and watch from down below while I do it."

Her head jerked up as if he'd struck her. "Cass, I can't! It's cruel to ask such a thing."

"Well, sweetheart, you've sure been laying the spurs on me."

Gayle stared at him. "I think it's time for me to go."

Suddenly, Cass realized he was driving her away. Wasn't he ever going to learn to control his tongue? Leaning forward, he propped his elbows on his knees and looked pleadingly up at her. "Don't go, Stormy. Maybe we can step back a pace or two and come at this from a saner angle."

She shook her head. "There isn't any point. When we come together, there is no sanity."

"Look, we both let our tempers get overheated. How

about it if I come over and see you tomorrow evening? Maybe by that time we'll have cooled down enough to talk."

Tears glazed her eyes, brimming over to run down her cheeks in silvery tinsel streaks. "Cass, it'll never work between us. So please don't come over, and don't call—it'd just make everything harder. We've said it all tonight. We don't have anything more to say to each other."

A chill colder than the lake water generated in his heart and spread through his body. "No, you don't mean that, Gayle, sweetheart. I won't let it be over!"

"There isn't anything you can do about it—that's the way it is."

The finality in her voice froze him so that he couldn't respond instantly when she whirled around and ran out of the house. He felt as if he were moving in slow motion when he jumped to his feet. By the time he'd reached the porch, the engine of her car had roared to life. "Stormy, wait!" he yelled, but if she heard, she ignored him, and headed down the drive-way with a spurt of gravel. "Gayle!"

After she'd driven out of sight, he plodded back into the house and stared around his living room. The last vestiges of her perfume were fading. The fire was dead already. The silence and emptiness hit him like a physical blow.

Suddenly, he realized what his house was lacking to make it a home. His blues and grays needed the bright female colors of Gayle, her copper and peaches and cream, to balance them out. And he desperately needed her warmth and love to balance him out. But he'd gone ahead and lost her, and now he'd never be complete again.

Turning his face toward the high ceiling, Cass gave a roar of grief and frustration.

Eleven

Gayle was almost home before reality sank in—everything was over between her and Cass. When it did, she began shaking so badly, she could barely steer her car into the garage.

Standing on the driveway, she stared up at the black sky filled with stars like great icy diamonds. "Why did you let this happen?" she whispered, bewildered and numb. Why send so incompatible a man into her life, taunting her with a taste of paradise, only to grab him away again? But she knew no celestial force was at fault. She was the one who had rushed willy-nilly into an impossible affair with Cass.

Crying out softly, she also knew she was the one who had broken them apart. How could she have picked so poor a time to throw their phobias in their faces? She should have known they were strung too taut on wired emotions after the accident to cope with a conflict.

Why had she pushed them to a point of no return? Wouldn't it have been better to live with love and dread than without Cass in an eternity of nothingness?

Gayle plodded heavily up onto the porch, which had been rebuilt by Cass, and walked into the living room where they'd made love on the floor. She wandered into the kitchen they'd refinished together. His laughter, his teasing, his energy and strength, were all imprinted everywhere in the house. And on her. Her very clothes were marked with his lifeblood. Taking her jeans and sweater off, she huddled under the bedcovers and wept bitter, hopeless tears.

Hours later she fell into an exhausted sleep. For the first time in weeks her nightmares came back. And this time the trauma victim she dreamed about was Cass, bloodied and broken. She awoke trembling and bathed with perspiration.

After hours of wakefulness she decided her only salvation was to leave Hamilton as soon as possible.

Cass had his stitches taken out at the hospital emergency room a week later, timing the procedure so that he could walk into Hilda's Home Health office at 4:30 P.M. Perching a hip on her desk, he dispensed with his usual screen of idle conversation and got right to the meat of his visit. "How's Gayle?" he asked.

"She looks about as peaked and miserable as you do, except for the shiner," Hilda said, peering at the greenish-black discoloration that had spread from his laceration to his eye. "You'll never learn, will you?"

"Apparently not. Do you suppose she'll be coming in pretty soon?"

"I suppose she will. But she gave me strict orders that she doesn't want to see you, should you happen to come around. Why don't you go home and call her?"

His shoulders drooped, and his heart sank. "Don't

you think I've tried to call her? A hundred times, and I only got through once—when she told me not to call again. Now she's got her damn phone on an answering machine, and I can't get through at all. She won't answer the door when I come to her house. And she's better than a CIA agent at covering her tracks when I try to intercept her around town. What am I going to do, Hilda? I'm desperate." He got up and jammed his hands into his jeans pockets, pacing around the office.

"She sounds just as stubborn as you are." Hilda studied him sympathetically for a moment, shaking her head slowly. "You really did it up good this time, didn't you Cass?"

"I sure as hell did."

She thought for a moment. "Gayle wouldn't want me to say anything, but I think you should know she handed in her letter of resignation."

He halted in midstep and whispered an obscenity. "But she can't leave. She's—" He stopped short of telling Hilda Gayle was his love, his world, his life.

"I'm afraid she can and will. If you want her to stay, you'd better do something quick. She's leaving in less than two weeks."

"What the hell can I do if she won't talk to me?" Cass roared, running his fingers desperately through his hair.

"Knowing you, I'm sure you'll think of something."

Gayle was sitting in front of Bonnie's desk at Ritz Realty, handing over the papers her mother had signed and sent back to her, finalizing the sale of the house to the rancher and his wife. "I want to get the flooring contractor in this week," she said. "So you'd better contact those people about choosing their own colors and the like."

"I'll do it right now." Bonnie made the phone call and hung up, grinning. "They'll be out within the hour to look the situation over."

"Good." Gayle sighed deeply. "The sooner this is over, the better I'll like it. I can't wait to get out of that place."

Bonnie's eyes sparkled. "I don't suppose it's any of my business, but are you planning to move in with Cass? Lucky girl, that house of his is—"

"Don't, please!" Gayle broke in. Her heart felt like glass breaking inside her chest. "It's over between Cass and me."

"Oh, no, don't tell me that!" Bonnie groaned. "What happened?"

"I don't want to talk about it."

"Okay, but what do you intend to do, then?"

"What I should have done three months ago, instead of coming here," Gayle said bitterly. "I'm going back to Portland and talk to a counselor. Then maybe I can get over this trauma phobia of mine and pick up my life again. I've wasted too much time hoping it'll go away by magic."

"But I'll miss you if you leave!"

"I'll miss you too. And everyone. I'll miss the town and the valley, and even the mountains."

Tears rose in Gayle's eyes when she realized that somewhere along the way the valley had become home, and its people her people. She felt guilty over leaving the patients she'd become attached to—they'd come to depend upon her. She'd promised to be there when Harvey "passed over." Who else would understand and sympathize with his grumbling? "You don't know how much I hate to leave, but I just can't stay and watch Cass flit from girl to girl. I'm sure you can understand that."

Bonnie gave an understanding nod. "Sure, but if you stay, you might meet another Jackson."

"I'll take my chances on meeting him in Portland," Gayle said, knowing no other man could ever take the place of Cass in her heart.

Bonnie sighed and leaned her elbows on the desk. "What are you going to do with the things in your house?"

Gayle snorted a laugh. "Most of my uncle's things are one step up from junk. I'll probably hire someone to cart them to the dump."

"Don't do that! Have a garage sale. People around here love that sort of thing. It'll be fun. Jackson and I will help you clear out the house before the carpet people come, and price things as we put them in the garage. It'll keep your mind occupied and off your troubles."

"Well . . . maybe it would. And I suppose it would bring in a few more dollars for my mother."

"Great, I'll put an ad in the paper for you. Since you're leaving in two weeks, we may as well schedule it for the weekend before the end."

When Gayle got home that evening, she had a panicked feeling that everything was snowballing and happening too fast. She felt lonelier than she ever had in her life. And she didn't even have any remodeling tasks left to occupy her. She stared at the blinking light on her answering machine and wept as she listened to Cass's voice alternately pleading and raging at her to return his calls.

After erasing the tape, she badly needed comfort and nurturing. She dialed Portland. "Hi, Mom."

"Gayle, darling, it's you! I'm so glad you called, I have wonderful news."

"So have I." She leaned her hips against the mint-quality countertop and crossed her feet. "The house is sold, and I'm coming home in two weeks."

"Oh, that's so wonderful! I can hardly wait for you to get here. I have someone I want you to meet. That's my big news—I'm getting married."

"You're *what*?!"

A delighted laugh came through the receiver. "It was a surprise to me too. I met Howard a month ago, and we hit it off right away. He's retired and very well to do, and so wonderfully generous. He insisted I quit my job immediately. Now we're having so much fun making travel plans. We're going to Europe on our honeymoon, and when we come back, we'll build a dream house. Everything is just perfect. And the wedding, darling, we're going to . . ."

Listening numbly as her mother went on and on, Gayle tried very hard to be happy for her. But every word, every facet, of the marriage plan seemed to be a weapon attacking her heart; she'd wanted all that so badly with Cass. She wondered why other people never seemed to have problems working out their love affairs. It wasn't fair.

Or was it a love affair? When her mother had finally ended her litany of plans, Gayle said, "You make everything sound wonderful, Mom, but I haven't heard you mention love."

There was a short pause. "Darling, I loved your father, and ended up terribly hurt. I like Howard, and we suit each other well enough." She quickly changed the subject. "But I haven't given you a chance to talk about what's happening in your life. I'll bet you'll be happy to get back home again, won't you?"

"Yes, I guess, sort of—I have mixed feelings," Gayle said, tightening her fist on the receiver. Mixed feelings! She didn't think she'd ever be happy again. "I've got to go now."

After hanging up, she stared at the phone. It occurred to her that all the work she'd done on the house was now a waste of time! What did a few thousand dollars mean to her mother with Howard in the picture? If she'd known that was going to happen, she wouldn't have come to Hamilton and had her heart broken.

"It isn't fair!" she cried out. "It just isn't fair!"

The day of the garage sale dawned clear and bright. After showers nearly every day, the fields were vivid with green grass and wildflowers blooming in profusion. The mountains were naked of snow against the sky. Canada geese were flying noisily around and around the valley in an excited flock of some hundred courting honkers.

Bonnie and Jackson arrived an hour before the sale was scheduled to help space the furniture out for the prospective buyers. All the smaller things were placed on borrowed card tables set up in the driveway.

At nine customers began driving up. To Gayle's surprise she'd inadvertently arranged one of the major social events of the season. She'd become so well known in the last three months that people came in droves out of curiosity and friendliness. They gathered in groups to discuss the weather and crops, neighborhood and world news.

Quite a few of the people bought merchandise. Even the bed and dining set sold, but would stay in the house until Gayle was ready to leave. Soon all that was left were a mismatched jumble of chipped dishes and dented kitchenware, and a dresser with two broken drawers. And two perfectly horrible table lamps her uncle had made himself.

At eleven things were still going so strong that Gayle didn't notice when Cass arrived. She looked up after a sale, and he was there, in what she called his lumberjack outfit: jeans tucked into work boots, red suspenders, blue plaid flannel shirt, and his red cap. He was laughing and teasing as he pawed through tableware with a couple of elderly women. He kept glancing at his watch every few minutes.

She groaned inwardly. It hurt so much to see him acting as if their separation hadn't affected him in the slightest, while her need for him made her feel as if all her life forces had been drained.

A customer came up, and Gayle turned away to the cashbox. When the transaction was finished, she looked up to find Cass next in line in front of the card table. His cap was cocked to the side, and he had the two atrocious table lamps in his hands. Up close, she saw that his face was drawn behind his cheerful grin. There were dark smudges under his eyes, and his tan looked a little sallow, the pink scar standing out. She wanted to cry, knowing he missed her too. "Hi," she said, surprised that her voice sounded normal. "I didn't realize you did garage sales."

"Oh, sure, auctions too. You never know when you might find something of unique value." He glanced at his watch, then held up the lamps. "A buck apiece, huh?"

She gave a flustered laugh. "Oh, for heaven's sake, you don't want those."

"You don't know a thing about what I want," he said quietly, his grin evaporating. Putting the lamps down on the table, he dug two dollars out of his pocket. "Are you making your mother rich?"

"Just about rich enough for a dinner out." Gayle held the dollar bills in her fingers, imagining she could feel a trace of him on them. "At least everyone seems to be having a good time."

"That's something." Cass checked his watch again, then hooked his thumbs in his pockets. "Did you know the bitterroots are blooming on your hillside?"

"Bitterroots? No—I don't even know what they are."

"Want me to show you?"

She glanced around at the gabbers and browsers who appeared not to be but certainly were watching, listening, and wondering what she'd do. He leaned forward to whisper, "Once again you're damned if you do and damned if you don't, but if you come with me, at lest you can be damned in private."

Giving a snort, Gayle tucked away the money and handed the cashbox over to Bonnie. "Show me those bitterroots, then."

Behind the house she clambered down the gravelly hillside beside him, through mossy rocks, wild grass, weeds, and wildflowers. Cass squatted down to sit on one heel, touching a forefinger to a pair of daisylike pale pink flowers growing flat to the ground. "This is a bitterroot."

Gayle went down on her knees. "That's *all* there is to the famous bitterroots? They're lovely, but I would never have noticed them if you hadn't pointed them out."

"The hillside's covered with them," he said, looking first at the sky, then his watch, then out over the slope.

She followed his gaze to his watch and to the cloudless sky, and to the slope, where she picked out dainty pink blooms all over the rocky spoil. "Why would anyone name a whole valley after such insignificant flowers? Why not after something showy and beautiful like an Indian paintbrush, or black-eyed Susan?" Her eye caught on some tall blue-gray weeds with purple thistlelike blooms. "Or even after those damned knapweeds?"

"Knapweeds aren't native." Cass puckered his chin and pushed up his mouth. "And I sure hope for your sake that someday you figure out showy beauty isn't synonymous with value."

Gayle felt her hackles rising. "What do you mean?"

"You figure it out," he said, and glanced impatiently at his watch.

Shifting to his other heel, he began one of his nervous monologues. "The Flathead Indians didn't see the bitterroot as insignificant, the roots were a staple in their diet. They came here in the spring to dig them and hold sacred rites, thanking their gods for the gift of the bitterroot. Now, have you ever known anyone to hold a dance for a black-eyed Susan?" He glanced at the sky and grunted impatiently.

Gayle studied his face, wondering why he was acting so strangely. "What point, exactly, are you trying to make?"

"I just thought you should see an insignificant bitterroot before you go back to Portland to your orchid family," Cass said, standing up to rub a cramp out of his leg.

He looked up with a mixture of relief and anxiety when a small plane came buzzing in from the northeast. Gayle looked up at it too. It was one of the biplanes that had been at the airshow. Just to the north of Cass's hill, across the valley, it began looping and diving, dragging a long streamer of white smoke. Her first thought was that it was out of control, perhaps on fire. But then it made another loop to finish off a perfect cursive capital L. "Why, he's skywriting!" she exclaimed.

"Yea-ah," Cass agreed, an odd tone in his voice.

The plane closed up a loop for an *o*, and dived into a *v*, then went into another loop for an *e*. Mouth agape with horrified embarrassment, Gayle watched the plane swoop and roll through a beautifully executed *Love you, Stormy* in giant white letters across the blue sky. For all the population of the valley to see!

A quick glance was enough to tell her all the people of the garage-sale crowd were standing on the crest of the hill, their heads bobbing as they divided their attention between the sky and Gayle and Cass.

"How *could* you deliberately make a spectacle of something that's hurting me so much?" she hissed, grabbing his arm.

"It wouldn't hurt so much," he hissed in answer, "if you weren't so damned stiff-necked."

"You're calling *me* stiff-necked!" she cried, then lowered her voice when she heard the murmur of voices cease. "You knew everyone would be here at my sale! How could you embarrass me this way?"

"Why in the devil do you think I did this to embarrass you?" he said, his eyes flashing. "I couldn't get in touch with you. Since you wouldn't listen to what I had to say, I damn well had to get my message across somehow. I do love you, and I don't care if the whole world knows it."

It suddenly occurred to Gayle that the plane was still writing—ascending, descending, and looping huge letters. She turned her face to the sky, mouth ajar, and watched silently until *Marry me* was spread across the heavens, signed with a flourished *Cass*.

That done, the biplane zoomed over the house, waggled its wings, and flew off toward the airport.

Cass lifted Gayle's limp hands and kissed them. "Now you've had an official offer. I'm asking you to stay here in the valley and marry me."

"I don't know what to say." Gayle felt topsy-turvy, wanting it so much but terrified of the implications.

Cass gazed down into her face with anxious brown eyes. "Just please don't say no right away. All I'm asking—begging—is that you stay in Hamilton for a while longer. Just long enough to try to work out some of our emotional junk."

She looked up at the sky, feeling as if her love, her longing, and her indecision were tearing her apart. The air currents had already distorted the letters until she could hardly make out the *Love you* any longer. She put her arms around him and pressed her face against his shoulder. "Cass, I'm afraid."

"I am too," he whispered, hugging her tightly.

"All right, I'll stay for a while, so that we can talk about us."

"Thank goodness. I'll call you tomorrow, when all this garage-sale ruckus is over." Cass pulled away and quickly climbed to the top of the hill, as if afraid to give her a chance to change her mind.

Gayle scrambled after him, oblivious to their audience. After he'd taken the dreadful lamps off the table and driven away in his pickup, she took a deep breath and turned toward the people watching her in question.

Everyone instantly turned away and began poking through the rubble left from the sale. No one was bold enough to ask what her answer to Cass's proposal had been. Which suited her fine, since she didn't know herself. But someone slyly suggested he'd never enjoyed a garage sale more. The others agreed. After a while they all left.

"Well, that's that," Bonnie said, bright-eyed, as Gayle piled coins into dollar piles. "This is a great day in the history of the valley. To my knowledge Cass has never proposed to anyone before. You couldn't turn him down, could you?"

Gayle glanced up. "There are a lot of snags to be worked out."

Bonnie threw up her hands impatiently. "But you and Cass are so perfect for each other—aren't they, Jackson?"

He squirmed in horror over being roped into an intimate discussion, but nodded his agreement.

"I appreciate your interest." Gayle stared at the piles of money. "But I'd appreciate it more if you'd butt out."

"You can't say no, because Cass—"

"Bonnie!"

"But—"

The sound of Jackson's voice shocked them both into silence. "Anyone with one eye and half a brain can figure out what ails you two," he said. "Why don't you just go climb the damn mountain with him and be done with it?" He gestured with his hand. "Let's go, Bonnie."

Openmouthed, Gayle watched them drive away. Maybe she had two eyes and no brain, because she couldn't figure anything out. Not how she could face Cass climbing his mountain on his own, much less how she could climb it with him. Or even what good it would do if she did.

Twelve

The garage sale had been exhausting. Her warring emotions after Cass's unique proposal had left her even more drained. Gayle had barely gone to sleep after falling into bed when the telephone jarred her into heart-thumping wakefulness again. The luminous clock dial said twelve thirty-five. Fumbling up the receiver, she answered and listened to Harvey's attendant say he was asking for her.

"Why, has he gone bad?" she asked, rubbing her bleary eyes.

"Not as far as I can tell, but he insisted I call you. He'll probably just go back to sleep, if you don't feel like coming out in the middle of the night."

Gayle hung up and yawned, tempted to wait until morning. But she'd probably just lie awake worrying about him anyway, if she didn't go. Slipping into a pair of jeans and a bulky gray sweater, she made the twenty-minute drive to his ranch.

"What's wrong?" she asked when she reached his bedside. He didn't look any more gray or short of breath than usual.

"Dunno . . . just a funny feelin' that I wanted you here."

"Let's have a look at you, then." His vital signs were stable, so she suspected he was lonely. Turning the lights down, she sat by his bed.

He beetled his shaggy white brows against the dim light. "Heard you had a wingding of a garage sale today."

Gayle smiled. "For a man who never leaves his bed, you have an amazing information network."

He nodded. "I also heard your house is sold. I 'spose you thought you could just up and leave before I pass over, didn't you?"

Now she understood why he'd called her—he was worried about being deserted. She'd promised to be there. How could she justify leaving, if she and Cass still couldn't work things out? She took his hand between both of hers. "I'll do my very best to be here."

He gave her a look. " 'Course you will be, you're here now, ain't you? Tonight's the night."

She knew better than to insist he'd be fine. "Yes, I'm here."

He nodded thoughtfully. "I been thinking about things endin'. I got me some regrets, I'll admit. I wish I could live my life over, all different. All I ever thought about was work, work, work, and save every cent. Don't fall into that trap, girl."

She didn't know how to answer him, so she remained silent.

He wheezed for a time, catching his breath. "What good's the money to me now? I should've taken my wife atravelin' while I still had her." There was a longer pause as he gazed up into the darkness. "I shouldn't have expected so much out of my boy."

"I didn't know you had a son."

"I don't. He ran off and got killed on the road in a car accident thirty years ago."

"I'm sorry."

"Not half as sorry as I am." He rested for a time, breathing harshly. "If I'd ever had a grandson, I would have wanted him to be like Cass."

"Yes, he's special." Gayle tucked a third pillow behind his back.

"I heard how he proposed. How you gonna answer?"

She stared at him for a moment, then said quite honestly, "I want to say yes, but I'm not sure we can work things out."

"He's a good boy."

"I know."

He gave an exhausted sigh. "My main regret is that I wasted my opportunities. My life has been dull as mud."

"I haven't found you a bit dull." Gayle leaned forward to kiss him on the forehead. "Especially at one o'clock in the morning. Why don't you go to sleep now?"

"Damn redhead, always pushin' people around." He squeezed her hand, then closed his eyes and drifted off to sleep.

The eastern sky was faintly pink, pushing back the dark at four-thirty, when Gayle drove back to town. Shivering and teary-eyed from the cold and from exhaustion, she ached for warmth and solid comfort. There was one place where she knew she could find those two things.

Driving up the hill, she parked in front of Cass's place. He never locked up, so she eased the front door open, wincing when a hinge squeaked, sounding like a shriek in the silence of the slumbering house. Tiptoeing down the hall, she stopped in the doorway of his bedroom. She didn't intend to awaken him. It was enough to know he was there, as big and strong and permanent as one of the mountains he wanted so badly to climb.

The room was almost dark with the blinds drawn. All she could make out in the oversize bed was the shape of a large man, spread-eagled on his back. He'd kicked off his covers, and the red thermal bottoms he wore for pajamas looked black in the faint light. His soft snoring sounded so cozy and homey, she began crying again. She clapped her hand over her mouth, just a second too late to muffle a sob.

Cass shot up to a sitting position. "Who's there?"

Gayle pulled in a deep, quivering sniff. "Me."

"Me, who?" He peered through the gloom, swinging his legs off the bed. "Stormy, is that you?"

"Don't get up." She walked quickly forward and sat down beside him, snuffling. "I didn't mean to wake you up."

He leaned sideways to pull several tissues out of a box on the table, and handed them to her. "What are you doing here?"

"I don't know," she said, blowing her nose and wiping her face.

Lifting his feet back on the bed, he folded his long legs Indian-style. "If you came to watch me sleep, it must've bored you to tears."

Her nervous laugh caught in the middle. "It wasn't boring, since you snore."

"I do not."

"Yes, you do—I liked it." She took a deep breath and laid her hand on his knee.

He picked it up and clasped it between both of his. "For the love of mud, you're cold as ice, Stormy. Where've you been—in a deep freeze?"

"Something like that," she said, shivering.

Cass got up and pulled off her shoes, then lifted her onto the bed, bulky sweater, jeans, and all. She was so tired, she couldn't resist, not that she wanted to. Slipping under the covers, too, he tucked the feather comforter up around her neck. Pulling her close to his sleep-warmed body, he folded his legs around her cold feet.

She huddled against him, soaking in the warmth and scent of him she'd missed so badly after their breakup. After a bit she began to feel warmer, but no less emotional. Tears came to her eyes, and to her disgust she began crying again. Cass held her, patting and shushing her while she sobbed. When the tears began to subside, he reached out and snagged another handful of tissues.

Gayle mopped her face. "Sorry, I don't know what's gotten into me. I've never cried about something like this before. It's just that I'd begun feeling he was more like a friend than a patient." She hiccuped another sob.

"Who?" He tucked the covers in around her shoulders.

"Harvey—he died tonight," she said in a voice thick from crying.

"Oh, damn," Cass whispered, pressing his face into her hair. He was quiet for a moment, then he began to snuffle too. That set Gayle off again, and for several minutes they held each other tightly and cried together.

A few minutes later he reached out and brought the whole box of tissues in bed with them. Rolling onto his back, he honked his nose and said, "I didn't realize I'd feel so bad over losing that old buzzard."

Gayle turned onto her back and honked her nose too. "He was a lot more loving than he wanted anyone to know. He thought of you as the grandson he never had."

"Yeah, I did see him as sort of a grandfather. Maybe because in the later years he didn't have anyone of his own either. He was always there, prickly as a wild cucumber, whenever I felt lonely and needed someone." He wiped his face. "I hope his end wasn't too hard."

"No, he just, well . . . passed over, like he kept saying. We talked for a while, then he fell asleep. A little while later he quit breathing."

Cass pressed his hands over his face for a moment, then said, "He was such a lonely old man. I wish I could have been with him. I'm glad you were there at least."

Gayle gave a shudder, thinking how close she'd come to not going; she would never have forgiven herself. "I think he called me because he thought I was going at my life all wrong. He's been trying to tell me that for weeks, and he wanted to finish getting the message across. But you know the way he always talked all around things. And I was too dense to figure out his meaning—if there really was one."

Cass laughed softly. "That's Harvey for you."

"Maybe, but darn it, he said only just enough so that my whole life seemed to come to a head while I was sitting with him. Now I can't trust anything I used to believe, and I feel lost."

Cass turned on his side, laying his leg over her knees and his arm over her waist, nestling her closer to his broad, hairy chest. "As long as you're in this bed with me, then, baby, you're not lost, you're found."

"That's one of the things I've begun to realize." She curved her hand around the morning bristle on his cheek. "I do belong here with you, despite everything."

"Oh, sweetheart, thank God for old Harvey if he got that across to you," he whispered, kissing her palm.

She lifted her head and kissed him on the lips. "I

always knew it, darling, but I'm only just now getting my priorities straightened out."

"Want to tell me about this upheaval of yours?" He bunched his pillow under his head, so he could see her better. The advancing sunrise highlighted the pink scar over his eyebrow and his fading black eye—battle scars of his own emotional upheaval.

She nodded. "Harvey talked about his regrets and all the things he was too frightened or busy to do. And I began seeing myself in him. Work, work, work . . . and afraid to trust people and love."

The very thought of it brought the exhaustion of a sleepless night crashing down around her. Pressing her face into Cass's shoulder, she whispered, "I can't bear thinking of myself at eighty, sick and all alone with nothing but my regrets to remember."

He wrapped his arms around her. "Believe me, Stormy, you're never going to be alone. And there's a big difference between you and Harvey."

"I'm not so sure. You know how important being a Critical Care nurse has always been to me?"

"The fighter pilot of nursing," he murmured.

She made a face. "I can't believe I said such a stupid thing! What conceit. Cass, I felt more fulfilled after holding Harvey's hand tonight as he passed over than I ever did after saving a life. Now I'm wondering if I ever was cut out to be a Critical Care nurse. I'm too squeamish."

He gently stroked her tangled hair. "Why'd you go into it in the first place?"

Gayle wrinkled her brow and thought for a while. "I guess because it made me feel important. As if I was somebody. Because I felt like a nobody in my family, and had to work two hundred percent harder than anyone else to justify my existence." She curved her lips in a crooked smile. "My mother accuses me of trying to save the world single-handedly."

Rosy light seeped in around the blinds, softening

the bold features of Cass's face as he curled his fist under his cheek. "Right—like giving up months of your life to fix up a house for her. Is she an impoverished, rickety little old lady in need of a white knight?"

"No, not hardly." Gayle tucked her fist under her cheek, too, and gave a laugh. "She told me the other night that she's found a rich man who's eager to support her in far greater luxury than she ever had with my father. Life seems so easy for beautiful women like her and my sisters."

A "gotcha" glint lit his eyes, as if he'd expected her to say something like that. "Tell me, if beautiful women have it so easy, how come your father divorced your mother? Was the other woman even more beautiful?"

She stared at him for a moment. "Well, no, she isn't by half, actually. That warrants some thinking, doesn't it?"

Cass reached out and curved his hand around her cheek. "You don't have to prove yourself, Gayle. You're the most special, caring, complete, lovely woman I've ever met."

Gayle saw her plain face and fairy-kissed freckles doubly reflected in Cass's eyes, made beautiful by his love. Her lip began trembling. Tears flowed, but with happiness this time. "You're a sweet, sweet man."

"Yea-ah, and don't you forget it," he whispered, grinning. "Why don't you let the world worry about itself and start living it up with me? I'll bet I can guarantee you won't die with regrets like Harvey."

She wiped her eyes with a clump of sodden tissues. "If I live it up with you, I doubt I'll ever reach the age Harvey did."

Cass snorted a laugh. "There is always that possibility."

He wound a tress of her curly hair around his finger, his face going sober and introspective. "I've been trying to understand myself, too, but I'm not having as much luck as you."

She curled an encouraging arm around his solid waist, debating how to respond. Once before she'd gotten them in trouble by pressuring him to talk about his feelings; she didn't intend to do that again. "Would you like to tell me how far you've gotten?" she asked cautiously.

He swallowed audibly and hesitated for a few moments. Then he said in a low voice, "Barely far enough to acknowledge the fact that I am . . . paralyzed with fear over climbing. And yes, I have been bashing around, thinking I could prove I'm not a coward." He glanced up her. "I purely do hate having you know I'm not the man I should be."

Gayle pulled his head down on her shoulder. "Good grief, Cass, you've been scaring the begessus out of me with your manliness ever since I met you." She ran her hand down his body, then put it around his waist again, slipping her fingertips into the elastic band of his thermals. "Besides, you've been proving your masculinity in other ways that impress me a heck of a lot more than those high jinks of yours."

He laughed, a soft, relieved sound. "You don't know how badly I needed to hear you say that. But be that as it may, I talked my problem over with a couple of my buddies from Search and Rescue. They were more understanding and sympathetic than I ever expected, and they're willing to talk me back up the cliff in Blodgett Canyon."

Gayle's eyes snapped wide open when an almost painful stab of anxiety pierced through her. She swallowed around a walnut-sized lump in her throat and forced herself to say, "When?"

He hesitated. "Well, I haven't exactly set a date yet. When I get everything organized, I guess."

If he was still having a hard time actually facing the

climb, so was she. When she swallowed again, the lump seemed to have grown to the size of an apple. "I'll be there to back you up, darling, any time you're ready," she managed to say.

"That isn't necessary," Cass said, shaking his head. "I only threw that challenge at you because you were pushing me and I wasn't ready to think about climbing yet."

"Oh, darling, I'm so sorry I did that," she said quickly, covering the new scar over his brow with her fingertips. "We were both so upset that night, and I broke us up. I caused us so much unhappiness."

"What makes you think you were the only one to blame? I acted like a royal jackass. Besides, I'm glad you told me what you thought. It was the truth, and I needed a good boot in the rear to jump-start my thinking."

Gayle put both arms around him, hugging tightly. "Maybe, but I can't bear to think that we might never have gotten back together."

"But we did, and here we are." Cass hugged her and thought silently for a few moments. "Half the reason I smeared my proposal all over the sky in front of you and the world was to force myself into working out our problems. And to do that, I have to climb the cliff. It'll probably take a nuclear blast to get me up there, but I imagine my S and R buddies will be glad to provide that."

Gayle threaded her fingers into his sun-streaked hair and clenched her fist gently. "I am going to be with you in the canyon, no matter what you say," she said with quiet determination. "If you're ready to face your fears, then I damn well better face mine too."

"Okay," he agreed after a moment. "I wouldn't dare chicken out if you were there."

Gayle loosened her fingers and studied his face. "Help me understand how you feel, darling. I *need* to know! What is so important about climbing a mountain? What draws you so?"

Cass turned over onto his back and pulled his knees up under the covers, frowning thoughtfully. "How to explain? I'm not sure I understand myself, exactly. There's the challenge, of course—like I'm always telling you. Pitting myself against something difficult and winning."

He turned his head and gazed at her, his dark eyes gleaming. "Even more important than that is the beauty of it, Stormy. It's breathtaking to stand on the top of a mountain and be able to see for hundreds of miles. It's as if you can see to infinity, with the miraculous earth spread out below—forest, rivers, sometimes even beyond, to the plains and the towns. You can stretch out your arms and say, 'I own everything my eyes can see! This is mine.'"

Gayle smiled at the rapt expression on his face. "And that's terribly important to you? That sense of owning the world?"

Cass pursed his lips for a few moments, as if reluctant to answer and reveal too much of his feelings. Then he took a deep breath. "From the time I was eight and lost my father, I never had anything that was my very own. As good as everyone in this town was to me, all I ever had were 'sort of' homes and secondhand families. I was the odd kid out—nothing and no one really belonged to me." He wrinkled his brow as if reliving old hurts, then glanced at her. "And that, Stormy, is the truth about why I love standing on top of a mountain and owning the world."

She ached for the little boy who must have felt so lost and alone. Putting her arm over his chest, she hugged him close. "Then we'd better get you back up there, hadn't we?"

Thirteen

Two days had passed since Gayle and Cass had talked. She should have felt happy and optimistic about the future, because for the first time they'd been open and honest with each other. She felt certain they could build a relationship now.

But instead of optimism, a terrible sense of premonition had begun plaguing her. The last time she'd felt it, Cass had split his head open. And now he was actively making arrangements to climb the cliff. What if he fell again and—

"Don't even think it!" she whispered fiercely, driving back to town from one of her final patient visits. She was planning to continue working for Home Health, but her sense of impending disaster had prevented her from telling Hilda.

It was easy for Cass to overcome his fear, she thought, all he had to do was climb up and over it. But how could she neutralize hers for him, when she so dreaded watching him put himself into dangerous situations? Would she struggle with these feelings over and over, for the rest of their lives?

After thinking all around the issues, she wondered

if more experience with mountains and climbing would help her overcome her horror of them. If she went back to the canyon and examined the cliff, surely she could talk sense into herself. Yes, that was it. Facing her fear was a beginning at least. Maybe this time familiarity would indeed breed contempt.

A few minutes later Gayle was perched on the edge of Hilda's desk. "Is it okay if I take the afternoon off?"

"Can't wait to get away from us, huh?" Hilda said with a good-natured smile.

"Not really." Gayle smiled, her eyes sparkling. "I haven't told you, but Cass and I are together again."

"Oh, I am so glad! I hope that means you'll be staying with Home Health too."

Gayle frowned. That niggly little warning voice inside was still stopping her from saying yes. What if . . .

"I don't know yet. Cass and I still have lots of things to work out. That's why I want the afternoon off. I'm going to Blodgett Canyon and take a look at the cliff that's caused us so much trouble."

Hilda frowned. "You wouldn't do anything foolish, would you?"

Gayle snorted. "I've never done a foolish thing in my life."

She went home and put on white shorts, a shell-pink T-shirt, and her hiking boots. When she arrived at the canyon, there weren't any cars in the parking lot, and no people in the picnic area or campground. That suited her purposes perfectly. She needed to be alone to face her bogeyman.

Everything except the wall of granite looked benign and inviting. Dainty white clouds floated in a sky so blue, it crackled. A crisp, clean breeze stirred the pine scent of the trees. The aspens were leafing out in a fresh yellow-green, and the stream was rushing with a merry roar.

Gayle walked slowly along the trail at the base of the cliff, skirting boulders and rubble that had been falling since the beginning of time. She located the pinnacle where Cass had been injured, and looked up at the light-colored area where the patch of rocks had broken off. She shuddered over the idea of him going up again. What if . . .

Nipping the "what if" in the bud, she clambered over the rubble until she had to throw back her head to look up at the wall. It was close to being perpendicular, but there were numerous handholds and ledges. "Huh," she whispered thoughtfully, "it really doesn't look so difficult to climb."

Maybe if she went up just a few yards, she'd conquer her fear for Cass. Cocking a leg, she jammed her boot into the first toehold.

At twelve-thirty Cass tracked Hilda down in the clattering, crowded hospital cafeteria. "Do you know how I can find Gayle?" he asked. "I had a notion to have lunch with her."

"She took the afternoon off. Says she wants to go rambling around Blodgett Canyon."

"Blodgett?! With who?"

"Alone, I guess."

"Why in hell would she go there alone?" he asked, his chest clutching.

Hilda looked up at him with some curiosity and more than a little concern on her face. "She was talking about looking at the cliff and problem-solving. I expect you'd understand better than I what that means."

He bit his lip. "You don't think she'd—"

Breaking off, Cass cut and ran for the door. Fifteen minutes later he parked next to Gayle's compact and jumped out of the pickup. She wasn't anywhere in sight.

"*Stormy!*" he shouted.

Echoes bounced back at him off the cliffs. His hands began shaking, and his breath speeded up. He had to turn his back to the cliffs, feeling as if he might suffocate.

Surely, she'd just gone up to the pool where they'd had the picnic, he told himself, and began walking toward the trailhead.

Then he stopped when something inside him raised a clamor. He didn't know how, but he felt she wasn't at the pool. With a sinking sensation he guessed exactly where she was, as positively as if she'd told him herself.

Adrenaline spurting into his system, Cass ran along the trail at the base of the cliffs in enormous strides. Every few minutes he stopped to cup his mouth and call her name. "*Gayle!*"

Finally, he heard a faint answer, almost drowned out by the noise of the stream. "I'm here, Cass."

He stopped and looked all around the wooded floor of the canyon, hoping against hope that she hadn't done what he knew in his heart she had. "Where, Stormy?" he shouted. "I can't see you."

"Up here," came the answer. "Look up."

He closed his eyes. Moments passed before he could bring himself to lift his head and look up. When he did, his heart dropped to the pit of his stomach. She was sitting on the pinnacle where his accident had happened, some twenty-five feet above ground. The white and pink of her clothes and the copper of her flaming hair made a brilliant contrast to the new gray granite where the rocks had fallen. The adrenaline had made his senses so acute, he could even see the glint of sunlight on the gold jewelry at her neck and ears.

In his mind Cass heard the rifle-cracking explosion of the avalanche splitting away. The rumble of its fall. He felt again the awful sense of not being able to breathe under the weight of the rocks piled on him.

"Stormy, no . . . not you," he said with a moan, his mind's eye putting her in his place. His love for her filled his heart and soul to bursting. He'd lost everyone he'd trusted and held dear. He couldn't bear to lose her too.

The fact that she was in danger drove everything else out of his mind. Leaping from boulder to boulder across the rubble, he began clawing his way up the cliff. He wasn't dressed for climbing; the blunt toes of his work boots slowed him down as he jammed them into crevices. His fingertips felt numb and fumbling as he hooked them into cracks.

It seemed like forever before Cass reached the top of the pinnacle and slung one long, jean-clad leg over the saddle behind it. The adrenaline of fear for Gayle was surging through him. It erupted in the form of blazing anger. "What in hell are you doing up here, Stormy?!" he roared, the words rebounding back and forth off the cliffs.

"Don't you start bellowing at me, Starbaugh!" she shouted in an echoing answer.

Then she had the audacity to laugh. *Laugh!* "Cass, you did it!" She grabbed his face and kissed him.

Too much anxiety was still pumping through his system to assimilate either her words or her kiss. "Dammit, answer me! What are you doing up here?!"

"Facing my phobias, darling. And it worked. I don't think I'll ever worry about your climbing again. This *is* fun!"

"Fun! *Fun!* Didn't I tell you this area is too fragile for climbing?"

"Well, yes, but I looked it over and decided it should

be safer than anywhere else. You already knocked down the unstable stuff last February."

"For the love of mud, there isn't an iota of logic in that assumption! How in hell do you think you're going to get back down?"

"Cass, I'm not stupid—I mapped out the return trip before I ever started up."

"You mapped out the . . ." he repeated faintly, staring into her sweet, precious face just inches away from his. She wore no hat, and he could literally see the fairy kisses popping out on her cheeks. He loved every one so much, he felt like crying. "Stormy, sweetheart, I thought my heart would leap out of my body when I saw you up here. All I could think was that you might fall and—"

Wrapping his arms around her, he pressed his face into the warm skin at the curve of her neck. She curled her arms around him, kissing his hair and the back of his neck. "You made it, Cass," she whispered against his ear.

"Made what?"

"You're up on a mountain again."

He lifted his head and frowned at her. Then he looked down at the rubble of boulders below. The stream, the pool, and a fluffy blanket of treetops waving in the breeze: The world was at his feet. He felt no panic, just exhilaration. And a wonderful sense of freedom. "Be damned if I'm not!" he said wonderingly, then scowled at her. "Oh, Lord, please don't tell me you risked your neck to con me back up onto this pinnacle."

"Of course not, you weren't even supposed to know I came here." She smiled at him. "Now that you've come this far, you shouldn't have any trouble going the rest of the way to the top."

Cass glanced up at the top of the cliff, jutting out

against the blue sky. His eye picked out niches and ledges, a crevice there, a crack there. It wasn't an impossible climb, just plenty difficult enough to be stimulating. "Interesting thought—I'd be tempted to try it right now, if I were dressed for it."

Then he looked at the love shining in Gayle's face. "Except that I'm a hell of a lot more worried about getting you down off here than going upward."

She clicked her tongue. "Cass, I can make it! No problem."

He clicked his tongue in answer. "All right, show me then—if you're so smart." He swung his leg off the saddle and descended a few feet. "But I'm going first, so I can catch you when you find out it's not the snap you think it is."

"That's fine," she said with laughingly labored patience. "But I'm not going that way. The route I mapped out is down the other side of the pinnacle."

Swinging her long, shapely legs over the other side, she began picking her way from toehold to fingerhold on a route Cass hadn't even considered. When he finally caught up with her, she was at the bottom. "You might have told me you were half mountain goat," he grumbled, feeling empty with relief now that she was safe. "Why didn't you just pop up to the top of the cliff yourself, and show me up properly?"

"Maybe I will someday—after you teach me everything I need to know about climbing." Gayle reached out her hand, and when he took it, she jumped to the boulder he was standing on.

He pulled her into his arms and gazed down into her remarkable gray eyes. "As long as we're here, how would you like to hike up to the place where we picnicked before?"

"Oh, yes, let's—I'd love that."

• • •

Gayle stood beside Cass on the broad stone slab and looked up at the pinnacle she'd found the courage to climb. Something powerful had happened up there. Turning her gaze to the woodsy scene reflected in the still, amber water of the pool, she thought about the other time they'd come there. About the first time he'd kissed her, and about her insecurities. She could barely remember the woman she'd been before she'd met Cass.

Then she looked at the strength of his tall body in his lumberjack outfit. There were curves of fun and laughter in his face, though now his expression was intense and introspective as he gazed at the top of the cliff. "Do you wish you were at the top?" she asked.

He shifted, as if coming awake, and looked at her with melting tenderness. "No, I don't wish that, Stormy."

"You aren't still . . . intimidated by it, are you?"

"The word is scared," he said, grinning. "No, I'm not scared any longer, thanks to your shock therapy. I've been looking at it, and I discovered something peculiar has happened. The challenge has disappeared. I can honestly say I don't care if I ever climb again."

"Is that good or bad?" Gayle asked, studying him anxiously.

"I'm not sure. I used to want to go up there to own the world, but now it just looks lonely and cold at the top." Cass took her in his arms, kissing her gently and tenderly on the lips. "I don't have to go on top of a mountain for that any longer, Stormy. The world is here in my arms."

Gayle held him tightly and sighed deeply, as if she'd come home after traveling a long, long way. She felt so many things: warm, comfortable, dainty, and beautiful, and so very loved. So *in love.* "I'm glad we came back to where we first began," she said softly. "It's the perfect place to tell you yes."

Cass didn't say anything for a moment, but she felt his body tense expectantly. "Yes about what?" he asked against her hair.

"Yes, I want to marry you, my darling."

Cass drew a quick breath and tightened his arms around her. "Oh, honey . . . oh, sweetheart . . . Stormy. It's scary to feel as happy as I feel now."

Gayle looked up at him. "I'd never want to hurt you, darling. That's why I was so careful to be sure. Now that I've said yes, I'll never leave you."

He gazed down at her with melting brown eyes. "I suppose it's old-fashioned for me to feel so happy that you were a virgin when you came to me. You weren't *sort of,* but the real thing. Nobody came first—you're just mine, Stormy. So special to me."

"It's not old-fashioned, it's so sweet, I think I'm going to cry," Gayle whispered, burying her brimming eyes on his plaid flannel shoulder. "I'm so glad I waited for you, because you cared enough to make me feel beautiful and precious and . . . fairy-kissed."

"You'll always be absolutely perfect in my eyes."

Cass held her quietly for a moment, twining his fingers in her tousled flaming curls. "Look, I really feel I have to warn you. Maybe climbing isn't tempting me just now, but I can't promise I won't go running after some new challenge that might come along later."

She pressed her face against his chest and listened to the powerful beat of his heart. Then she looked up at the new scar over his brow. "I won't mind, darling. I've finally figured out that you do those crazy things because you love life so much, you want to live it to the fullest. Not because you don't respect your life, as

I first thought. I fell in love with a daredevil, Cass, and I don't want you to change. I want you to teach me to enjoy life as much as you do."

"Stormy, sweetheart, I—" When his voice broke, he tightened his arms and pulled her against him. Lowering his head, he kissed her all over her face and then on the mouth. First his lips were gentle with love, then demanding as desire flared. He ran his hands up under her T-shirt, exploring willing territory. After a few moments he lifted his head and looked down at her. "I swear, sweetheart, if I loved you any more, I'd just up and explode. Mmm-*hmmm*."

"Oh, darling, me too." She pulled his head down to continue the kiss. His vigorous response speeded up her pulse. Drawing back, she laughed softly. "Could it be that Mr. Gusto has joined us?"

"Mr. Gusto is hoping we intend to finish something we started here once before." He grinned, his face flushed. "Or is this place too public for your passion for privacy?"

Gayle glanced around. The little bower seemed wonderfully private with aspens and pines circled around, and the towering cliffs hovering protectively close, reflected in the placid amber pool. Still, there was always a possibility that someone might pop in off the trail.

After only a second's hesitation she laughed, drawing Cass toward a soft bed of pine needles under the trees. "Let's take a chance. There's nothing I like better than a good challenge."

Cass broke into a huge grin. "Yea-ah!"

THE EDITOR'S CORNER

What an irresistible line-up of romance reading you have coming your way next month. Truly, you're going to be **LOVESWEPT** by these stories that are guaranteed to heat your blood and keep you warm throughout the cold, winter days ahead.

First on the list is **WINTER BRIDE**, LOVESWEPT #522, by the ever-popular Iris Johansen. Ysabel Belfort would trade Jed Corbin anything for his help on a perilous mission—her return to her South American island home, to recover what she'd been forced to leave behind. But he demands her sensual surrender, arousing her with a fierce pleasure, until they're engulfed in a whirlwind of danger and desire. . . . A gripping and passionate love story, from one of the genre's premier authors.

You'll be **BEWITCHED** by Victoria Leigh's newest LOVESWEPT, #523, as Hank Alton is when he meets Sally. According to his son, who tried to steal her apples, she's a horribly ugly witch, but instead Hank discovers a reclusive enchantress whose eyes shimmer with warmth and mystery. A tragedy had sent Sally Michaels in search of privacy, but Hank shatters her loneliness with tender caresses and burning kisses. Victoria gives us a shining example of the power of love in this touching romance guaranteed to bring a smile to your face and tears to your eyes.

Judy Gill creates a **GOLDEN WARRIOR**, LOVESWEPT #524, in Eric Lind, for he's utterly masculine, outrageously sexy, and has a rake's reputation to match! But Sylvia Mathieson knows better than to get lost in his bluer-than-blue eyes. He claims to need the soothing fire of her love, and she aches to feel the heat of his body against hers, but could a pilot who roams the skies ever choose to make his home in her arms? The sensual battles these two engage in will keep you turning the pages of this fabulous story from Judy.

Please give a big welcome to brand-new author Diane Pershing and her first book, **SULTRY WHISPERS**, LOVESWEPT #525. Lucas Barabee makes Hannah Green melt as he woos her with hot lips and steamy embraces. But although she wants the job he offered, she knows only too well the danger of mixing business with pleasure. You'll delight in the sweet talk and irresistible moves Lucas must use to convince Hannah she can trust him with her heart. A wonderful romance by one of our New Faces of '92!

In **ISLAND LOVER**, LOVESWEPT #526, Patt Bucheister sweeps you away to romantic Hawaii, where hard-driving executive Judd Stafford has been forced to take a vacation. Still, nothing can distract him . . . until he meets Erin Callahan. Holding her is like riding a roller coaster of emotions—all ups and downs and stomach-twisting joy. But Erin has fought hard for her independence, and she isn't about to make it easy for Judd to win her over. This love story is a treat, from beginning to end!

Laura Taylor has given her hero quite a dilemma in **PROMISES**, LOVESWEPT #527. Josh Wyatt has traveled to the home he's never known, intending to refuse the inheritance his late grandfather has left him, but executor Megan Montgomery is determined to change his mind. A survivor and a loner all his life, Josh resists her efforts, but he can't ignore the inferno of need she arouses in him, the yearning to experience how it feels to be loved at last. Laura has outdone herself in crafting a story of immense emotional impact.

Look for four spectacular books this month from FAN-FARE. Bestselling author Nora Roberts will once again win your praise with **CARNAL INNOCENCE**, a riveting contemporary novel where Caroline Waverly learns that even in a sleepy town called Innocence, secrets have no place to hide, and in the heat of steamy summer night it takes only a single spark to ignite a deadly crime of passion. Lucy Kidd delivers **A ROSE WITHOUT THORNS**, a compelling historical romance set in eighteenth-century England. Susannah Bry's world is turned upside-down when her father sends her to England to live with wealthy relatives, and she meets the bold and dashing actor Nicholas Carrick. New author Alexandra Thorne will dazzle you with the contemporary novel **DESERT HEAT**. In a world of fiery beauty, lit by a scorching desert sun, three very different women will dare to seize their dreams of glory . . . and irresistible love. And, Suzanne Robinson will captivate you with **LADY GALLANT**, a thrilling historical romance in the bestselling tradition of Amanda Quick and Iris Johansen. A daring spy in Queen Mary's court, Eleanora Becket meets her match in Christian de Rivers, a lusty, sword-wielding rogue, who has his own secrets to keep, his own enemies to rout—and his own brand of vengeance for the wide-eyed beauty whom he loved too well. Four terrific books from FANFARE, where you'll find only the best in women's fiction.

Happy Reading!

With warmest wishes for a new year filled with the best things in life,

Nita Taublib

Nita Taublib
Associate Publisher / LOVESWEPT
Publishing Associate / FANFARE

Enter Loveswept's Wedding Contest

AH! WEDDINGS! The joyous ritual we cherish in our hearts—the perfect ending to courtship. Brides in exquisite white gowns, flowers cascading from glorious bouquets, handsome men in finely tailored tuxedos, butterflies in stomachs, nervous laughter, music, tears, and smiles. . . . AH! WEDDINGS!! But not all weddings have a predictable storybook ending; sometimes they are much, much more—grooms who faint at the altar, the cherubic ring bearer who drops the band of gold in the lake to see if it will float, traffic jams that strand the bride miles from the church, or the gorgeous hunk of a best man who tempts the bride almost too far. . . . AGHH!! WEDDINGS!!!

LOVESWEPT is celebrating the joy of weddings with a contest for YOU. And true to LOVESWEPT's reputation for innovation, this contest will have THREE WINNERS. Each winner will receive a year of free LOVESWEPTs and the opportunity to discuss the winning story with a LOVESWEPT editor.

Here's the way it goes. We're looking for short wedding stories, real or from your creative imagination, that will fit in one of three categories:

1) THE MOST ROMANTIC WEDDING
2) THE FUNNIEST THING THAT EVER HAPPENED AT A WEDDING
3) THE WEDDING THAT ALMOST WASN'T

This will be LOVESWEPT's first contest in some time for writers and aspiring writers, and we are eagerly anticipating the discovery of some terrific stories. So start thinking about your favorite real-life wedding experiences—or the ones you always wished (or feared?) would happen. Put pen to paper or fingers to keyboard and tell us about those WEDDINGS (AH)!!

For prizes and rules, please see rules, which follow.

BANTAM LOVESWEPT WEDDING CONTEST
OFFICIAL RULES

1. *No purchase necessary.* Enter Bantam's LOVESWEPT WEDDING CONTEST by completing the Official Entry Form below (or handprinting the required information on a plain 3" x 5" card) and writing an original story (5–10 pages in length) about one of the following three subjects: (1) The Most Romantic Wedding, (2) The Funniest Thing That Ever Happened at a Wedding, or (3) The Wedding That Almost Wasn't. Each story must be typed, double spaced, on plain 8 1/2" x 11" paper, and must be headed on the top of the first page with your name, full address, home telephone number, date of birth, and, below that information, the title of the contest subject you selected when you wrote your story. You may enter a story in one, two, or all three contest categories, but a separate Entry Form or Card must accompany each entry, and each entry must be mailed to Bantam in a separate envelope bearing sufficient postage. Completed Entry Forms or Cards, along with your typed story, should be sent to:

   BANTAM BOOKS
   LOVESWEPT WEDDING CONTEST
   Department NT
   666 Fifth Avenue
   New York, New York 10103

   All stories become the property of Bantam Books upon entry, and none will be returned. All stories entered must be original stories that are the sole and exclusive property of the entrant.

2. *First Prizes (3).* Three stories will be selected by the LOVESWEPT editors as winners in the LOVESWEPT WEDDING CONTEST, one story on each subject. The prize to be awarded to the author of the story selected as the First Prize winner of each subject-matter category will be the opportunity to meet with a LOVESWEPT editor to discuss the story idea of the winning entry, as well as publishing opportunities with LOVESWEPT. This meeting will occur at either the Romance Writers of America convention to be held in Chicago in July 1992 or at Bantam's offices in New York City. Any travel and accommodations necessary for the meeting are the responsibility of the contest winners and will not be provided by Bantam, but the winners will be able to select whether they would rather meet in Chicago or New York. If any First Prize winner is unable to travel in order to meet with the editor, that winner will have an opportunity to have the First Prize discussion via an extended telephone conversation with a LOVESWEPT editor. The First Prize winners will also be sent all six LOVESWEPT titles every month for a year (approximate retail value: $200.00).

   Second Prizes (3). One runner-up in each subject-matter category will be sent all six LOVESWEPT titles every month for six months (approximate retail value: $100.00).

3. All completed entries must be postmarked and received by Bantam no later than January 15, 1992. Entrants must be over the age of 21 on the date of entry. Bantam is not responsible for lost or misdirected or incomplete entries. The stories entered in the contest will be judged by Bantam's LOVESWEPT editors, and the winners will be selected on the basis of the originality, creativity, and

writing ability shown in the stories. All of Bantam's decisions are final and binding. Winners will be notified on or about May 1, 1992. Winners have 30 days from date of notice in which to accept their prize award, or an alternative winner will be chosen. If there are insufficient entries or if, in the judges' sole opinion, no entry is suitable or adequately meets any given subject as described above, Bantam reserves the right not to declare a winner for either or both of the prizes in any particular subject-matter category. There will be no prize substitutions allowed and no promise of publication is implied by winning the contest.

4. Each winner will be required to sign an Affidavit of Eligibility and Promotional Release supplied by Bantam. Entering the contest constitutes permission for use of the winner's name, address, biographical data, likeness, and contest story for publicity and promotional purposes, with no additional compensation.

5. The contest is open to residents in the U.S. and Canada, excluding the Province of Quebec, and is void where prohibited by law. All federal and local regulations apply. Employees of Bantam Books, Bantam Doubleday Dell Publishing Group, Inc., their subsidiaries and affiliates, and their immediate family members are ineligible to enter. Taxes, if any, are the responsibility of the winners.

6. For a list of winners, available after June 15, 1992, send a self-addressed stamped envelope to WINNERS LIST, LOVESWEPT WEDDING CONTEST, Department NT, 666 Fifth Avenue, New York, New York 10103.

OFFICIAL ENTRY FORM

BANTAM BOOKS
LOVESWEPT WEDDING CONTEST
Department NT
666 Fifth Avenue
New York, New York 10103

NAME _____

ADDRESS _____

CITY _____ STATE _____ ZIP _____

HOME TELEPHONE NUMBER _____

DATE OF BIRTH _____

CONTEST SUBJECT FOR THIS STORY IS: _____

_____

SIGNATURE CONSENTING TO ENTRY _____

_____